JIM

BY THE SAME AUTHOR

Boxy an Star

JIM GIRAFFE

a ghost story
about a ghost
giraffe

Daren King

Jonathan Cape
London

Published by Jonathan Cape 2004

2 4 6 8 10 9 7 5 3 1

First published in Great Britain in 2004 by
Jonathan Cape
Random House, 20 Vauxhall Bridge Road,
London SW1V 2SA

Random House Australia (Pty) Limited
20 Alfred Street, Milsons Point, Sydney,
New South Wales 2061, Australia

Random House New Zealand Limited
18 Poland Road, Glenfield,
Auckland 10, New Zealand

Random House (Pty) Limited
Endulini, 5A Jubilee Road, Parktown 2193, South Africa

The Random House Group Limited Reg. No. 954009
www.randomhouse.co.uk

www.jimgiraffe.com

A CIP catalogue record for this book
is available from the British Library

ISBN 0-224-06958 6

Papers used by Random House are natural,
recyclable products made from wood grown in sustainable forests;
the manufacturing processes conform to the environmental
regulations of the country of origin

Typeset by Palimpsest Book Production Limited, Polmont, Stirlingshire
Printed and bound in Great Britain by Mackays of Chatham plc, Chatham, Kent

For Sarah Maguire, who helped me

Contents

Topload Video

I have of late been visited by a ghost giraffe. He steps out nightly from the wardrobe, the only item of furniture tall enough to house him, and paces the room in long looming strides, sometimes with a pair of underpants on his head, sometimes not, and stops between my wife's bed and mine.

He began as a shapeless glow, as though someone had rigged up a strip light in the wardrobe and partially opened the door. Several nights later, a leg emerged, bony and long. Followed by three others.

Then, last night, I buttoned up my moon-coloured boxer shorts, stepped into my alien-shaped slippers, passed beneath the giraffe's legs and walked down the stairs to the kitchen, where I made myself a mug of cocoa. On my return I found him still there, looking a tad peeved. I kicked off my alien-shaped slippers and sat on the bed. He put his face close to mine, so close that I could smell the leaves on his breath, fresh leaves from the very tops of the trees, and spoke. Tomorrow, he said, I will visit you during the day. Your wife will be polishing the sideboard. You will have set up a topload video, and I will play you a tape. When I protested that our video was frontload, he explained that the tape was enchanted and was not compatible with some of the newer machines.

I take the afternoon off work, borrow an old silver-coloured video player from my parents, untangle the cables and plug it in. I keep expecting my wife to ask what I am up to, but she is busy polishing the sideboard, just as the giraffe had said. And here he comes now, through the patio doors, without even wiping his hoofs, a videotape clenched between his teeth. He opens his mouth, drops the tape into my hands, and says: 'All right, mate?'

'Yes,' I say icily, 'fine.'

'Not so scary in the day, am I.'

'And what makes you think you were scary during the night?'

'You were scared stiff first time you saw me.'

'No I wasn't.'

'You hid under the duvet, you old lamer.'

'I'm not old,' I say, straightening my top-of-the-range long-range spectacles. 'I'm twenty-eight.'

'Twenty-nine next birthday. Then thirty. If you make it.'

'What a grim thought. Not my making it,' I add quickly. 'The suggestion that I might not make it. Either way, it was a horrible thing to say.'

'Plenty more where that came from.'

'So I take it you haven't descended from the heavens to cheer me up.'

'I'm here to spook you, give you the creeps.'

'Well, you're going the wrong way about it. Assuming an earthly form, you got that bit right. But not as a giraffe.'

'Always been a giraffe,' the giraffe says. 'Wouldn't know how to be anything else.'

'Then if you must insist on haunting people, you should do it back in the jungle where you belong.'

He wrinkles his nose when I say this, that long yellow nose, and says: 'I'll tell you one thing, I'm beginning to wish I'd stayed in the wardrobe. You were scared when I was in the wardrobe.'

'Do you mind. I happen to be fearless.'

'Dickless.'

'That is neither accurate nor fair,' I say in my genitalia's defence. 'Do you know what I do for a living?'

'Surprise me.'

'Head Script Writer, Science Fiction Channel.'

'A writer, eh. Well, if you're so good with words, how come all that time I was in the wardrobe, you never even said hello?'

'You're a giraffe,' I say sensibly. 'Had I known you could speak—'

'If I couldn't speak, there'd be no point me coming here.'

'You sound like you're on some sort of mission.'

'Wouldn't have bothered descending from the heavens,' the giraffe says, 'if I didn't have something big to say.'

'Then get on with it, and get out.'

'Not yet. But believe me, it's heavy shit.'

'Ready when you are,' I say, settling into my high-tech armchair.

The giraffe just flares his nostrils, shakes his head. 'Don't feel like it.'

I rise from the chair. 'Then let's start with something easy. The name is Spectrum. Scott Spectrum.'

'Jim.'

'Nice to meet you, Jim,' I say, shaking his right front hoof. 'So tell me. How does it feel, Jim, to be a freak?'

'Eh?'

'There can't be many ghost giraffes stalking the earth.'

'Giraffes die too, you know.'

'All that lives must die,' I recite, 'passing through nature to eternity.'

The giraffe smiles when I say this. 'None of us is getting any younger.'

'Come again?'

'Well, Spec, it's like you said. All that lives must snuff it—'

'Is that where this is leading? You're here to remind me of my mortality?'

'Bingo.'

'With each passing year I grow closer to the grave. Then, when old and withered—'

'Steady. You're getting soppy, not to mention optimistic.'

'Middle-aged then, with all my imperfections on my head.'

'On the bog, your head in a porn mag.'

'Oh, I don't read pornography, Jim.'

'You should, while you've still got the chance.'

'So it's imminent then.'

'More or less, yeah.'

I just sit here, enjoying my high-tech armchair, recollecting a conversation from the previous night. I was watching television, a time-travel show, and my wife was watching the clock. She asked me why I never speak, and I said nothing.

'Cheer up, Spec. You're better off out of it. I mean, face it, what have you got to live for?'

'I assume you are being ironic. You happen to be looking at the man who has everything. High-speed internet connection. Beautiful wife—'

'Who needs a good seeing-to.'

'A good what?'

The giraffe winks, and the penny drops.

'Oh, you mean sex. Continence has no interest in it.'

The giraffe laughs. 'Continence? Continence Spectrum?'

'It's a beautiful name,' I say in the name's defence.

'Well, Continence Spectrum is in need of a good seeing-to. Would do her myself, Spec. If bestiality weren't illegal. And if my dick wasn't so big. And if I weren't dead.'

'Excuse me, but Continence and I happen to be in love.'

'Then why is your life so shit?'

'Fine,' I say, changing tack. 'Let us suppose. For the moment. For the sake of argument. That my life is, as you put it, shit. Which it isn't. And we both know it isn't. But if, and I stress again the word "if", my life is shit, then what in heaven's name do you intend to do about it?'

'Eh?'

'Wave a wand. Grant me three wishes. What?'

'You're stepping into the realms of fantasy now,' Jim says. 'I'm a ghost giraffe, not a fucking wizard. If you're going to be an idiot, Spec, I might just as well go down the pub and leave you to it.'

'Point taken. But will you please stop calling me Spec. You make me sound like a small spot or particle. My name is Scott Spectrum, or simply Scott. Now can we just watch the tape?'

He lowers his head, level with the silver-coloured video

player, and pops the tape in, pushing down the top with his chin. Then, in a clumsy attempt at pressing the play button, he starts hoofing the front of the machine. I point the remote control between his legs.

'Scott Spectrum,' he says, 'this is your life. Past, present and future.'

Fuzz. Then, the thick mist of a school playing field. Two boys emerge, one of whom I recognise as myself. That's me on the left, with the floppy fringe and spectacles. At my side is Tinpot Wheeler, the only boy ever to show me his willy. His tie is askew and two of his shirt buttons are missing. He puts his hand into his blazer pocket, pulls out a crisp and stuffs it into his mouth. 'Want one?'

'Yes please.'

'Prawn cocktail. Nicked them from my dad's pub.'

I take a bite from the crisp.

'You started wanking yet?'

I shrug.

'Slow starter, are you?' he says with his mouth full. 'Bet you have loads of wet dreams then.'

'I haven't wet the bed since I was eleven years old.'

'Not that sort of wet dream, you flid.' He picks pocket fluff from another crisp and stuffs it into his mouth. 'Do you know what spunk is?' He punches me between the legs and says: 'That white stuff in your balls. Comes out when you wank.'

'When you what?'

'Don't you even know what wanking is?'

Evidently not, for I shake my head.

'Must be a flid then. You know when you're in the bath and your mum comes in and you get a stiffy?'

I nod.

'It's called wanking. Ain't you never done it?'

'Not on purpose.'

He picks his nose, his finger reaching deep into his brain. The thing he pulls out looks valuable, a precious stone, but all he does is wipe it on to my blazer. 'You going to that party?'

'What party?'

'Lisa is having a party, at her house,' Wheeler says. 'Didn't she invite you?'

'No.'

'Ask her if you can go.'

I turn red, and turn away.

'You scared?'

'No.'

'Then ask her.'

'I'm not allowed out Thursday nights,' I state truthfully. 'It's bath night.'

'Don't be a wanker, you flid.' He punches me in the stomach and runs off.

The scene cuts to an afternoon geography lesson. Tinpot Wheeler and I are sat one desk from the back. Lisa is sat directly behind me.

The teacher taps the whiteboard with his pen. 'Capital of Egypt, anyone?'

I know the answer to that, surely I do, but I say nothing. Cut to a close-up of my armpits, damp with spreading maps of sweat.

Lisa leans forward and pokes Tinpot Wheeler with her ruler. 'Oi,' she whispers. 'You still coming to my party?'

Wheeler nods.

'Who else is coming?'

Wheeler elbows me in the ribs. 'He is.'

My body stiffens, awaiting the prod of Lisa's ruler, but no prod comes.

The teacher steps up to our desk. 'You know this one, Scott. Capital of Egypt.'

'No, sir.'

'What have you got there?'

'Nothing, sir.' But there is something. I'm hiding it under my hand.

'I do hope it is something geographical.'

Evidently not, for I scrunch it up and stuff it into my shirt pocket. Wheeler snatches it and stands up, waving it in the air. 'I know what it is,' he cries, unscrunching it. 'Love letter.'

The teacher is not amused. 'Give it here, Wheeler.'

'Lisa Lisa shining bright—'

'Wheeler, sit down.'

'— let me be your love tonight.'

The rest of the class are in hysterics, punching each other and calling me a flid, unaware, no doubt, that the word refers to victims of thalidomide, a morning-sickness drug found to damage the foetus.

I wipe the salt from my spectacles. 'It was a long time ago.'

'Soppy git.'

'It was a difficult time.'

Jim passes me a tissue. 'I don't know how you could hang around with that Wheeler boy. Zits the size of custard creams. Hairstyle you could have a fight with.'

'I wonder where he is now,' I say, glazing over. 'Doing time, one would imagine.'

'If you say that word just once more, I'm going to hoof you.'

'What word?'

'Time.'

'Now that is what we call a bad repetition.'

'Call it what you like,' Jim says haughtily. 'I call it a pain in the udders.'

'Then allow me to rephrase.' I compose myself, then say: 'I wonder where Tinpot Wheeler is now. In prison, one would imagine.'

Jim opens his mouth to speak, then closes it, shakes his head and says: 'I forgot what I was going to say now.' He trots off through the patio doors, turns round, and comes back in. 'Yes, the Wheeler boy. Just because he was a loser at school. People can change, Spec.'

'Now who's being soppy?'

He blushes at this, bright yellow, the first time I have ever seen Jim Giraffe blush. So he does have a sensitive side. I must work on that. He gives me a hard stare. 'You're the one bawling his eyes out.'

'Oh, and whose fault is that?' I say, claiming the moral high ground. 'Why would you want to stir up bad memories?'

'I'm trying to educate you, in the ways of the world.'

'Superfluous,' I say cleverly. 'I may have been awkward as an adolescent. But look at me now, look at my wife.' Which reminds me. Continence. Wherefore art thou. I rise from my high-tech armchair and look round. Hmm. 'It's a clever trick, Jim.'

'What trick?'

'Looping time.'

'Eh?'

'She was polishing the sideboard before we watched your film. End of part one and still she rubs. How do you do it?'

'Do what?'

'She is house-proud,' I say proudly, 'but no sideboard demands that level of attention.'

'What are you on about? Looping time, my hoofs. She's having a sexual fantasy.'

'She's polishing.'

'Rubbing.'

'Rubbing then. But what has that got to do with sex?'

'A lot if you're a woman. It's how they masturbate.'

'Jim, women do not masturbate.'

'Your wife does.'

'My wife has better things to do with her fingers.'

'What, like sew up the black holes in your space socks? The world has changed, Spec. Women want orgasms, and they want them now. And another one in a minute.'

'I know that, Jim.'

'Then why are you such a dickhead?'

I laugh. 'And what makes you think I'm a dickhead?'

'You use your head, Spec, when you should be using your dick.'

'But Jim, sex is dirty.'

'So is your wife,' Jim says, picking his nose with his hoof. 'If you paid her more attention, you would know these things.'

'Oh, I pay her plenty of attention.'

'You should dump her. The two of you have grown apart.'

'Our relationship has barely changed since the day we married.'

Jim pulls a face, wrinkling his nose and teeth. 'But you sleep in separate beds.'

'An arrangement which dates back to our honeymoon.' My eyes turn to the ceiling, which clouds over. 'Continence kept tickling me. I instructed her to stop, but she would insist on tickling me. So I built a wall out of pillows. Pretended they were sandbags. When she scaled it I retreated across no-man's-land to the sofa. Where I spent the remaining fortnight in a huff.'

Jim is staring at me, open-mouthed. 'Have you finished?'

I remove my spectacles, wipe them on my shirt. 'It is important in a marriage to lay ground rules.'

'No wonder you suffer from erectile problems.'

'Hardly,' I say, flicking my fringe.

'You don't even know what erectile problems are.'

'I do.'

'What then?'

'Erections. And they're a bloody nuisance. Get in the way when you're rummaging for change for the cocoa machine. Not sure why I still get them, I'm not even an adolescent.'

'You don't need to be an adolescent to get an erection, Spec. I've got one now, and I'm dead.'

'Oh, you haven't.'

'What do you think that is, a fifth leg?'

I peer beneath the giraffe's flank. Disgusting. And huge. It seems to be dribbling. 'Put that away, before my wife sees it.'

'Where do you want me to put it? Up my arse?'

'How about the back garden,' I say drily. 'Oh, Jim, why must you be so dirty?'

'Eh?'

'That's right, dirty. It's not just your mind, either. Look at the state of your teeth. And your breath carries a strong stench of nature. That's why I was afraid of you,' I say cuttingly, 'I thought you might breathe on me. Do you know what I used to say to myself, when this all started? Here he comes, I would say. Ol' Treetops Breath. Ol' Tree Breath.'

Jim just stands there. His long yellow-blue nose droops and his eyelids half close. Even his penis has gone flaccid, hugging his coconut balls. 'That hurts, that really hurts. Leaves act as a natural breath freshener. And as for teeth. Nothing wrong with my teeth.'

'I've seen rhinos with better teeth.'

'Bad example. This mate of mine, Barry, he's a rhinoceros. They have birds in their gobs, clean up all the shit. I'm very funny about my teeth, Spec.'

'I love it when you show your sensitive side,' I tease. 'Seen precious little of it so far.'

'Everyone's got a delicate underbelly. Don't mean you have to go and prod it.'

'Then I apologise. Though I do wish you would learn to open up a bit.'

'If I weren't a ghost,' Jim says eerily, 'I would wallop you on the kisser.'

'Oh, don't be so pathetic.'

'What about you, you boring git? I'm the only interesting thing ever to happen to you. If they made your life into a film, Spec, it would be all about me.'

'Then the film would never get made. You're unfilmable. Imagine the casting problems. Not to mention the budget. What with all those special effects.'

'A bloke could play me. Lanky, big hooter. Yellow make-up. Blue spotlight. Giraffe-pattern trousers and patent-leather high-heeled boots.'

'That could work.'

'Or try this,' Jim says dramatically. 'Starring Jim Giraffe, as himself.'

'You would need to cut back on the swearing.'

'Got to express myself.'

'I work for the Science Fiction Channel, remember. Talking of television,' I say, rising from my high-tech armchair, 'we ought to watch the rest of your tape.'

'Is that your answer to everything? Not now, Continence, I'm watching telly.'

'And who is that supposed to sound like?'

'You, you four-eyed git.'

'Jim,' I say archly, 'I do believe you are talking out of your snout.'

'Scott Spectrum, you have to be the most boring man I have ever bothered to haunt.'

Despite all the threats, it is difficult to be intimidated by a ghost that's giraffe-shaped. Funny how an animal so tall can fail to frighten one. Mice are scary, even to those of us who are not afraid of them, but a giraffe? Nothing scary about a giraffe, supernatural or otherwise. And that breath. Like leaves from the very tops of the trees. Fresh, yes. But strong. A friend of mine works as a tree surgeon, so I ought to know.

Fuzz. Then, Scott Spectrum, reclining in a high-tech armchair, watching a fly-in-the-ointment documentary about Scott Spectrum. When I raise my left hand, the televised Scott Spectrum raises his left hand too. Every detail is there, from floppy blond fringe and top-of-the-range long-range spectacles to graph-paper trousers and non-slip anti-static socks. No sign of Jim though. But Continence is there, in the background, rubbing the sideboard with all her home-making might. Her straight brown hair is tied back in a straight brown shape, tied with a round brown hair-tie. She polishes until the doorbell rings, polishes some more, then stops polishing and looks at me. Not the televised me, the real me. 'Scott, is it your turn to answer the door?'

Evidently not, for I shake my head.

'Well, I will get it this time,' she says, smoothing her long brown skirt, 'and you can get it next time.' We follow her down the hall to the front door. Zoom in on her hand, drawing the bolt, turning the handle, releasing the latch.

Cut to an extreme close-up of a battered working-class face. It's Tum, the single mum, and she's brought with her her newborn baby, Baby Bathwater. 'Cont,' she says, shortening my wife's first name to its first four letters, 'couldn't give me a hand, could you, Cont?'

'With what?'

'My baby. It keeps sicking itself. And sicking things up.'

'What things?'

'Funny-shaped bits of sick,' Tum says, passing Baby Bathwater to my wife. 'One bit come out like a lump, another bit like a lump of sick.'

Continence takes Baby Bathwater from Single Mum Tum and carries it through to the lounge. Tum follows, then runs back to close the front door. My wife lays Baby Bathwater on the carpet, steps over it, taking care not to step on its head, unfolds a tablecloth over the table, picks up Baby Bathwater and places it on the tablecloth on the table.

'It keeps sicking things up,' Tum says, catching her breath. 'I'm worried sick. Keep thinking to call the doctor. Thing is, I have to keep leaving the window open. The house smells of sick. Other thing is, Cont, what if my mum comes round? Give me a right piece of her mind, she will. The state of me.'

'Perhaps we should concentrate on the baby.'

'I better think of a name for it.' Tum lifts her maternity

dress and tugs at the cord of her knickers, and the cord attached to her tummy button. 'Might get a naming-a-baby book. Picture of a baby on it. Oi, now what you doing?'

'Saving your baby's life,' my wife says, removing an object from the baby's mouth.

'Typical. Slouched in front of the telly. A crisis on our hands and he don't lift a finger.'

This, I am ashamed to say, is true. My eyes have remained on the screen, even during the scenes featuring vomit.

Tum picks up Baby Bathwater and puts it over her shoulder. 'Typical man. What's he watching anyway?'

'It looks like some sort of drama.'

'Is that all he does all day? Watch telly?'

'It's research,' Continence says in my defence. 'He works for the Science Fiction Channel, don't you, Scott.' She says this with perfect clarity, but unfortunately I am too engrossed in the programme to hear.

'Mind you,' Tum says, kneading her swollen stomach, 'tend to watch a lot of it myself. What with a baby on the way. You should have a baby, Cont. Or don't he shag you?'

'I've stopped wanting him to,' Continence says, toying with her round brown hair-tie. She gives Tum a conspiratorial wink and says: 'I am having an affair.'

Now, nothing brings me to the edge of my high-tech armchair like a revelation of infidelity, and this revelation of infidelity is no exception. I wheel forward, my head so close to the television that I am practically eating the screen.

'His name is Leroy,' Continence says. 'He's very good in bed.'

'Have you told Scott?'

'Of course not. It wouldn't be an affair if I told my husband. Not that he would hear me over the television.'

'Have you tried swearing at him?'

'Not my style, Tum.'

'Can I have a go?'

'Be my guest.'

So the pasty-faced single mum stands behind my high-tech armchair and yells an expletive. When I fail to respond, she starts whacking me round the back of the head with the back of her hand.

'Don't hit him.'

'I'm trying to get a rise out of him.'

'Leave him,' my wife says firmly. 'He may be a geek but he is my husband.'

Tum takes a can of rape spray from her handbag, and prepares to discharge the noisy alert gas into my face. Continence attempts to disarm her, but the working-class woman looks back at her in anger and knees her in the front of her skirt. I ought to do something, turn off the television, rise from my high-tech armchair, drop the remote control and wrestle the proletarian to the carpet. But she is bigger than me, she frightens me, and besides, she makes compelling viewing.

Fortunately, my wife can take care of herself. She lifts Tum's maternity dress, snaps off her bra, scoops up a handful of milky mammary and drags her out into the street.

'What about my baby?'

'If you want it,' Continence says, 'you will have to bid for it. I'm putting it up for adoption.' And off she goes, Baby Bathwater in her arms, Single Mum Tum yapping at her heels.

'No wonder you need glasses,' Jim says. 'Sit back a bit.'

'Sorry, I just got really involved.'

'Make you think, did it?'

'No,' I say candidly. 'It was just good television. Shame about that horrible working-class woman though.'

'Nothing wrong with the working classes,' Jim says defensively. 'I'm working class.'

'Yes, and look at the state of you.'

The ghost giraffe shakes his head in disbelief. 'You really are a tosser. No wonder you never hug the wife.'

'I do hug her. Every evening,' I say, checking my mental schedule. 'While she does the washing-up.'

The giraffe raises an eyebrow. 'From behind?'

'My wife likes it from behind.'

The giraffe raises his other eyebrow. 'So I hear.'

'Oh, get back to the jungle, you filthy beast.'

Jim flares his nostrils. 'Racist.'

'How dare you call me a racist,' I state dramatically. 'If I had my stepladder to hand, I would climb to the top rung and throttle you. Or at least part of you.'

'All right, calm down,' Jim says, backing away. 'Keep on like that and you'll have a heart attack.'

'Never,' I say, beating my chest. 'I'm as strong as an ox.'

'A fox more like,' Jim says melodically. 'In a box. Wearing a chastity belt. On his snout. You're repressed, Spec, and it needs to be sorted out. It's all those hours you spend at the keyboard. Get some fresh air. Enjoy yourself, for fuck's sake.'

'Change the compact disc', I say satirically. 'Slow down, Mr Spectrum. Or you will bring on a coronary. This is old news, Jim.'

'And yet heart disease remains one of the world's biggest killers.'

'You sound like you've swallowed a pamphlet.' I scratch my spectacles. 'So what do you suggest I do?'

Jim shrugs. 'I just think you need to shoot your load once a week. Take the weight off your nads.'

'If you're suggesting I masturbate—'

'Everybody does it, Scott. Even God.'

As he says this, my mouth drops open and one of my teeth moves. 'Did you just say what I think you said?'

'Eh?'

'So it is true.'

'Steady,' Jim says. 'All I meant—'

'It all makes sense now,' I say, putting two and two together. 'There must be a God, else you wouldn't be here.'

'Well, even if there is, I don't believe in him.'

'So you're an agnostic.'

'Sarcastic.'

'Sarcastic then. You believe that the existence of God is not provable.'

'Put it this way. If he does exist,' Jim says, twitching his ears, 'He's a bum chum.'

'A what?'

'A bum chum. A poof.'

'You can't say that.'

'Bearded cunt.'

'Jim, please—'

'Anyway,' Jim says, cocking his leg and urinating into the coal-effect electric fire, 'all I was saying was, if you don't sort yourself out, take things easy, you'll end up like me. Bitter and twisted. And dead.'

'How do you mean?'

'Like I said. You're on your way out. Heart attack. Any day now.'

'You're serious, aren't you.'

'Look at my face,' Jim says blankly. 'My poker face, this

is. Of course I'm serious. Your days are numbered. There's a funeral bill somewhere with your wife's name on it. Continence Spectrum, for the burial of her husband Scott. Fifty quid, special offer.'

Even as the giraffe speaks, I can feel my blood turning to clotted cream, my arteries filling up with fudge. I jump up, grab the telephone and dial.

'Who are you calling?'

'Everyone.'

'Calm down. You don't need to call anyone. Not yet anyway.'

'So there is a chance?'

'Of course there is. That's why I'm here.'

'To save me?'

The ghost giraffe nods.

'But why?' I enquire, putting down the receiver. 'You don't even like me.'

'I died the same way myself. And believe me, it wasn't nice.'

'What happened?'

'There I was, running around the jungle, sticking my neck out and that sort of caper, when I snuffed it. Heart failure.'

'But you're a giraffe.'

'Giraffes fuck up too, you know.'

'But according to you, Jim, heart attacks are brought on by heavy commuting.'

'Not in the jungle.'

'So what did cause it?'

'The wrong kind of leaves.'

'Nonsense.'

'Spiky ones. I choked on them. And when a giraffe chokes, it puts a strain on the heart. Well, you try pumping blood up a ten-foot neck.'

'Must you mention blood?'

'So I ended up in giraffe heaven. And a right load of rubbish it is too.'

'How so?'

'They just don't have the facilities. No trees, for one thing.'

'What would you need trees for?'

'To stick my head up.'

'Well, could you not stick it up something else?'

'Like what?' Jim says wryly. 'My arsehole?'

'Impossible.'

'Not if you're bored enough.'

'And did you?'

'I tried. It's the ears. And these funny little horn things,' Jim says, lowering his head. 'So I thought, sod this, and came back down to earth.'

'But you said you came here to help me.'

The ghost giraffe goes quiet for a minute, then says: 'All right. What happened was, I started out doing haunting. Boo-to-a-goose sort of caper. Just having a laugh. Then, some old wheezer kicked the bucket. Died of shock.'

'Oh dear.'

'The-laughter-turns-to-tears sort of caper.' He flares his nostrils. 'Fuck this, I thought. I need a holiday. So I hid in your wardrobe.'

'And that is your idea of a holiday?'

'A change is as good as a rest, Spec. Trouble was, I got bored. And when a ghost giraffe gets bored, it sees the future.'

'Naturally.'

'I saw yours, Spec. And there wasn't a lot of it.'

'So you decided to do something about it? To be my saviour?'

'Bingo,' Jim says, grinning from ear to ear. 'That's what I am, a saviour. A sort of cocky version of Jesus.'

I return to my high-tech armchair. 'Well, I appreciate the

gesture, but you aren't doing a very good job. All this talk of my life being shit. It hardly fills one with the joys of living.'

'Yeah, sorry about that. The main thing is, I gave you the tip-off. Follow my advice and you'll live to die of old age. Or in traffic. But keep this up. All those long hours. And it's curtains.'

A decision, then. One big enough to knock either one of my non-slip anti-static socks off. I lean back in my chair, and listen. To the clock. As it ticks my name. Scott. Scott. Scott. Each tick representing a beat of my heart. A beat which could be the last.

A decision. To live like Jim. Or die.

'If I do pass away, what will happen to my wife?'

'I'm glad you said that,' Jim says, grinning from ear to there. 'Let's watch the rest of the tape.'

Fuzz. Then, the splash of black tyres on wet black tarmac. Wide shot of a black hearse, pulling up outside a suburban cemetery. In its back, a coffin, inside which, I presume, is me. Or what is left of me. For I am dead.

Slow dissolve to the seminar room of the local planetarium. Above the stage, a galaxy of stars forms an image of my face, my spectacles, my fringe. Beneath this, the coffin, along the lid of which pace the soft shoes of the planetarium director, who pauses momentarily to gaze out upon row upon row of seats. And I have to say, it's quite a turnout.

First row, left to right. My mother, her nose red, her eyes redder. My father, his head in a magazine, reading in extreme close-up— or is he asleep? My brother, biting his finger. My sister, whose husband is in prison for fingering his eldest daughter. His eldest daughter, who is the daughter of my sister. My sister, who— no, we've done her. My grandmother on my father's side, sobbing her heart out into a hanky and holding it up and wringing it out. My grandfather on my mother's side, trimming his beard with a pair of shears. A friend of the family, who wishes to remain nameless. My best friend, Vic Twenty, of whom more later. My boss at the Science Fiction Channel, Harry Maker, dressed in his attention-seeking silver suit, his necktie a sliver of silver, his shirt a screen-printed collage of photographs taken from his bedroom window. He's got his, um, partner with him, Doctor Bang, author of the best-selling popular-science book Why Blood Is Sticky. And there's Spot Plectrum, founder of the Scott Spectrum Fan Club. That isn't his real name, by the way. He changed it because he wanted to be like me. He even dresses like me. Oh, and there's Jim Giraffe, back row, second left. You could spot him a mile off. It's that smug grin.

The second, third, fourth, fifth and sixth rows are filled with science-fiction fans. I recognise some of them from conventions, but it's their T-shirts that really give them away. Most depict our most popular show, Space Man In Space. Even Jim is wearing one. It features a hologram of Space Man— that's the name of the hero in Space Man In Space— and above that the Space Man In Space logo. If a T-shirt wearer were to turn round, we would be able to read the slogan: In Space, No One Can Hear Space Man In Space Scream In Space. I thought that up. Catchy.

The planetarium's director paces the length of my coffin once more, stops, coughs, looks at his watch, shakes his head, and says: 'Shall we give her five more minutes, then make a start? Otherwise we shall be here all night.'

'Continence wouldn't be late for my funeral,' I protest. 'Do you think I have not heard of editing? I work in television, remember. The whole thing might have been produced on a computer. For all I know, it could all be another of your illusions.'

'What illusions?'

'Oh, come on. One minute you are able to fit inside a wardrobe—'

'I can explain that. What I did was, I threw out a load of your stuff. Your old sports kit, and that box of used bus tickets.'

'How dare you tamper with my memories.'

'And your school project, that papier-mâché space station. That went on next door's skip.'

'What I was trying to say,' I say, trying to hide my hurt, 'before you so rudely interrupted, was that I am fully aware of your extraterrestrial powers, particularly with regard to scale. You possess powers not of this earth, and therefore cannot reasonably expect me to believe everything I see in one of your videos.'

Jim says nothing to this. He paces the room in thought, turning in ever decreasing circles. This is not easy for a giraffe, but as I said, he has these powers. He clears his long throat – a long process – and says: 'You know when you're trying to think of a word, and you can't quite put your hoof on it?'

I adjust my high-tech armchair, increasing my comfort level by upwards of eight and a half per cent. 'Try me.'

He thinks once more, only briefly this time, then says: 'What do you call that thing where they wave the flags?'

'The coronation.'

'Not as soppy as that. When someone is trying to land a plane, and the bloke on the runway waves these flags to tell the pilot one of the wings has fallen off.'

'Semaphore,' I say brilliantly. 'A system of signalling using two flags. You can do it with your arms.' And much to Jim's surprise, I can do it with mine. He watches transfixed as I semaphore the phrase 'ghost giraffes are silly'.

'Semaphore, right.' He nods, pleased. Then shakes his head. 'But not that. A bit like that, but not that. Something to do with something to do with poems.'

'You should never semaphore a poem, Jim. It loses all its subtlety, its little nuances.'

'I mean when you write a poem and it's about something, but it's really about something else.'

'Metaphor.'

Jim's whole face lights up, bathing the entire room in a warm yellow glow. I should get him some fluoxetine. Save a fortune on the electricity bill. 'That's it, Spec. Metaphor.'

'I must say, Jim, I never thought of you as a poet.'

'Never mind that,' Jim says, swatting away the soppiness with his tail. 'The point is, the video was a metaphor, not to be taken lightly.'

'Literally.'

'Not to be taken literally.'

I nod. 'Then how should it be taken?'

Jim shuffles his nostrils, organising his thoughts. 'Your wife will be there to see you off, but her mind will be on other things.'

'All right. Then let us just say. For the sake of argument. That I follow your instructions. I get out more. I perform sexually for my wife. With the television off. I do these things, and the heart attack is averted. What will happen to you?' I kneel by the old silver-coloured video player and eject the tape. 'More saving? Or back to giraffe heaven?'

Jim bats an eyelid. 'Nothing that soppy. I get rounded up. And shot.'

I hand him the tape. 'Oh? And why is that?'

'Penalty for doing a runner.'

'Well, that's a bit harsh,' I say in the ghost giraffe's defence. 'You die, and then they shoot you. Talk about kick a mammal when he's down.'

'Not really.' He tosses the tape on to the sofa. 'Put me out of my misery. Bullet between the eyeballs and wham, it's all over. No more of this living-in-limbo caper.'

'But how can they shoot an ethereal being?'

'With big fucking bullets.'

Not much I can say to that. What do you say to the giraffe who has nothing. Who has risked his long neck to save your short neck. By offering you a bunch of half-baked advice. 'Well, it was nice to meet you, Jim.'

'Hang on,' he says, as I usher him into the hall, 'I want to ask you a favour. How about putting me up for a few nights?'

'I thought you said you were going to be shot?'

He grins. 'They'll have to catch me first.'

'But a moment ago you were ready to give yourself up.'

'I may be a giraffe, but I'm not stupid. I'm going AWOL. Absent without leaves. So what do you reckon? Come on, mate, it's only a few nights. Just till I get myself sorted out.'

I scratch my chin, then shake my head.

'What about your spare room?'

'You mean the utility room. There isn't room. In the utility room. Unless, of course, you happen to be a utility.'

'I could stay at your sister's.'

'You would bring on her asthma.'

'I could sleep with her daughter, her little girl.'

'Jim,' I protest, 'she's a child.'

'Children like animals.'

'But you're perverted.'

'All right, I can take a hint.'

'Don't forget your enchanted videotape.'

'Keep it,' Jim says. 'Anal git.'

'Oh, don't be like that. Look, wait till Continence gets back from the adoption agency. See what she says.'

He shakes his head.

'Stay, illusion!'

'Cock off.'

And with these rude words, the ghost giraffe is gone.

Stretch Armlong

Having been disturbed by the ghost giraffe every night for two full weeks, it is now his very absence I find disturbing. The slightest glimpse of his long nose would have me out like a light. After several impatient hours, I climb out of bed, open the wardrobe door and peer inside. Nothing, not even a token heap of dung.

My wife's duvet makes turning-over noises and she sits up, rubbing her head, making it make that familiar squeak. 'Scott, what are you doing?'

I close the wardrobe door and return to my bed. 'I heard a noise. I thought it might be an intruder.'

'In the wardrobe?'

'Yes,' I say. 'Or. Um. A shirt.'

'A shirt.'

I nod.

'Scott, is there something on your mind?'

I shake my head.

'Are you having problems at work?'

Again, I shake my head. My wife has a black belt in body language, and can easily read my gestures, even in the dark. I lie on my back, my eyes to the black space where there really ought to be a ceiling. 'Continence, you know when you polish the sideboard. Does it make you feel, um. Excited?'

'You do say the funniest things.' I listen as she fluffs up her pillow, props it against the wall and sits up. 'Does it make me feel excited? Well, I do enjoy it. As with any repetitive task, it allows the mind to wander.'

'Where does it go, when it wanders?'

'Nowhere really. I might be lying in a field. I kick off my shoes and wriggle my toes at the flowers. Yes, and then I look up and there is this horse, a rippling black stallion. And it tears off my skirt with its teeth.'

'How rude. What happens next?'

'It climbs on my back and rides me.'

'Surely you mean the other way round? You hop into the saddle and take hold of the reins as it trots off across the paddock.'

'No, it is definitely the horse who rides me.'

'How unusual.'

'It is a very unusual horse.'

I nod. Just as I thought. It is nothing but a perfectly innocent flight of fancy. Jim Giraffe was wrong. Which reminds me. 'Continence, do you believe in ghosts?'

'No I don't.'

'How about really tall ghosts?'

'Oh, Scott, you really must get some sleep.'

I feel silly now. For the first time tonight, I am glad of the dark. If you are going to feel silly in front of your wife, you might as well do it in the dark. I wait for her breathing to slow, then cross no-man's-land and slip beneath the duvet and hold her. I hold her with all the hold I can muster. For it would seem that I am not long for this world. And can hold her only on a temporary basis.

I almost drift off myself, but then the room turns yellow blue and guess who.

As a boy, I would never go to school without first making my bed, fearing that I would return home to find it stuffed full of ghosts. The moment Jim appears, I instinctively dash across the room and draw my duvet over my mattress.

'You soppy bastard.'

'What?'

'I just caught you two hugging.'

'We were conserving heat.'

'Conserving heat my udders,' Jim says sardonically. 'I hope you're going to hump her. No point warming her up if you don't take a ride.'

'She's a wife, not a motorbike. No wonder they call you Mr Cynic.'

'Eh?'

'Affection is an end in itself, Jim, not a means to an end.'

'Rubbish.'

'And you were wrong about the sexual fantasy. All that nonsense about masturbating with the sideboard. She was frolicking. With a horse.'

'I bet she was.'

'It rode on her back. A bit topsy-turvy but that's my Continence.'

'Let me show you something,' Jim says. 'Turn the light on.'

'She might wake up.'

'Chuck a pillow on her head. This is important. If this doesn't give you a heart attack,' Jim says ominously, 'nothing will.'

I get out of bed, fold my wife's duvet over her face and switch on the bedside lamp.

'Open the drawer.'

'If this is about my odd socks—'

'Your wife's drawer.'

'No,' I protest, 'I never invade her privacy.'

'This is part of your problem. Open it.'

I do. It contains her smalls.

'Rummage around at the back, see what you find.'

I do, and retrieve something thick, long and hard. 'Oh,' I exclaim, holding it up. 'What is it?'

'A dildo.'

'In my wife's drawer?'

He nods.

'This is ridiculous,' I say, waving the dildo at the ghost giraffe. 'Did you put it there? Do you know something, Jim? If my wife sees this she will be physically sick.'

'You prat,' Jim says pitifully. 'It belongs to your wife. She bought it at Adam & Eve.'

'Adam and whom?'

'Adam & Eve, the soppy sex shop.'

'Continence would never buy a thing like this.'

'She would, Spec. And she did.'

'But it's huge,' I say, marvelling at its great length. 'And. It's black.'

'Think about what she said earlier, about having an affair. She mentioned a name. Do you remember what it was?'

'Leroy.'

'A black man's name.'

I look at the thick, rubber-coated object. It's so big, I have to hold it with two hands. Both of which are shaking. Causing it to vibrate. As though switched on.

'Look at it,' Jim says. 'That's Leroy.'

I shake my head.

'Scott, meet Leroy. Leroy, meet Scott.'

'This is unbelievable,' I say open-mouthed. 'So she really is having an affair. In a sense.'

'Adds up now, doesn't it. The sideboard. The daydream.'

'No, she definitely got rode by a horse.' But as the words come out, I realise what they mean.

'Did she tell you the horse's colour?'

'Black.'

'I think you better put him back now,' Jim says gently. 'You don't know where he's been.'

I return Leroy to my wife's smalls and close the drawer. 'Thanks for telling me this, Jim. It means a lot to me.'

'Where are you going?'

'To bed,' I say, getting into bed. 'Busy day tomorrow. Brainstorming the new series of Space Man.'

'But I have to show you something.'

'You just did.'

'Something else.'

'There is nothing you could show me after that. It would pale into insignificance.'

'Think again.' The giraffe backs up, turns, and trots out through the wall.

I get out of bed, pull on a Space Man T-shirt, slip into my alien-shaped slippers and follow, silently closing the bedroom door. By the time I locate the landing light switch, Treetops Breath has already reached the hall. As I descend the stairs, the wallpaper turns floral and I find myself in the home of my parents.

'Wait here,' Jim says, passing through the lounge door.

I crouch on the floral carpet and put my left spectacle lens to the keyhole. I can see my father, hunched up in his armchair, shuffling a pack of cards. What is he playing at, playing cards at this hour? And more to the point, what does he intend to play? Patience, one would assume. A game for one player. Or pairs, with my mother, who is in the kitchen making cocoa, or stretched out along the sofa eagerly awaiting her next hand.

I open the door and go in, only to find that things are not as I had thought. What I had taken to be the light of the little floral lamp is actually the glow of the television. And the person sprawled out on the sofa is not a person but a certain ghost giraffe. He looks at me, winks. 'Gay porn.'

'What?'

'Gay porn. Your dad is a closet poof.'

Oh my. He isn't shuffling cards at all. He's masturbating.

'No sudden moves. You don't want to rupture the force field or whatever you call it. This is your dad's favourite tape, Spec. No wonder he wanted his video back. That boy there, with the white bum. He's only fourteen. The old man is buggering him.'

'But why?'

'Don't ask me,' Jim says defensively. 'I'm a healthy mammalian heterosexual.'

'But Jim, why would my dad watch a gay film? He's a married man.'

'A married gay man.'

'But he's my father. How can he be gay,' I say naively, 'if he's had children?'

'He wasn't gay back then. It all started last year, when he met Flynn.'

'Flynn who?'

'Flynn who he stuck his willy up. You remember when your dad quit that job at the pacemaker makers?'

'He was made redundant,' I correct, 'due to downsizing.'

Jim shakes his head. 'They needed a trainee, so they brought in this school leaver. Your dad had to teach him how to work that machine, the one that makes the pace-makers.'

'The pacemaker-making machine.'

'That's the one. Every time Flynn bent down, he would brush his arse against your dad's hand, and before you could brush your hair with a hairbrush, it was your dad's hand doing the brushing. Flynn suggested they meet for a drink, and they did. And then. They did it.'

'Did what?'

'It.'

'Oh.'

'In the pub toilet. Flynn on all fours, your father at the helm.'

'And then what?'

'Flynn went home. He had to be up early, for work. Not your dad though. He stayed till closing time, then went and told your mum.'

'About Flynn?'

Jim shakes his head. 'About the pigeons.'

'What pigeons?'

'The mutant pigeons.'

'What mutant pigeons?'

'The ones that invaded the factory, forcing it to close down. They even ate his redundancy cheque.'

'And she believed him?'

Jim shrugs. 'Anyway, the whole thing was forgotten. Then, a month ago, your dad started buying these tapes.'

'I suppose he gets them at that sex shop.'

'You won't find these at Adam & Eve, Spec. He gets these from a bloke in the pub.'

'And why is this one his favourite?'

'The boy in it looks like Flynn. We better get out of here. Your dad is about to shoot his load.'

I step back into the hall. No son should ever witness the fruit of his father's loins. Or is it the other way round? Either way, I don't fancy an eyeful.

Back in the hall, Jim instructs me to turn off the light.

'But why?'

'You want to go home, don't you?'

I sigh, and flick the switch.

For a moment, Jim just stands there, glowing smugly like the big yellow show-off that he is, then he says: 'Now turn it back on.'

I do. Oh. 'Jim, this is my sister's house. You said we were going home.'

'Did I?'

'Well. You implied that we were going home.'

'Who cares.'

'I do, for a start. I'm tired, Jim. I want to go to bed.'

'I have to show you something.'

'Not again.'

The stairs are varnished wood, and, as you know, wood has a tendency to clomp. Fortunately, Jim's hoofs are made of ghost and my alien-shaped slippers are heavily padded, so we reach the top in near silence. Jim stops at the door to my sister's eldest daughter's bedroom and says: 'Follow.'

'You keep away from her, you filthy beast.'

'Do what I say. Or discuss it with the business end of my hoof.'

'Right, I'm going home.' I mean it, too. I'm going home, even if I have to walk all the way in my alien-shaped slippers.

Jim watches me for a moment, then bites his lip, his eyes rolling backwards into his brain. 'Look, I'm sorry if I seem tetchy—'

'You don't seem tetchy, Jim. You are tetchy.'

'Spec, this is important. You might actually learn something.'

'There is nothing you could teach me about our Pinky.'

'She has periods.'

'Jim, thirteen-year-old girls do not have periods.'

'They do, Spec. Big ones. How else would they get out of school sport?'

'What are you doing?' He's poking his nose through Pinky's door.

'Come on,' Jim says, withdrawing. 'She won't even know you're here. I've done a magic spell.'

'I thought I could smell something.'

'That was my fart. I've also done a magic spell, to make you invisible. Wait till I've gone through the door, then let yourself in.'

'Jim, I—'

'Are you worried she might be up to something?'

'Certainly not,' I say, perhaps a little louder than necessary. 'She has school tomorrow. She will be fast asleep.'

'Then you have nothing to worry about.' Jim gets about

three-quarters through the door, then backs up, looks me right in the face, and says: 'Follow.'

Having little choice, I open the door and step inside.

'Why does night have to be so dark,' I complain. 'I can't see a thing. Not that there's anything to see.'

'There is, Spec. Come closer.'

'No thanks.'

'Suit yourself, but you're missing all the fun.'

'Jim, there is nothing fun about sleeping. Not even a novelty nightie can see to that.'

'She isn't sleeping, Spec. She's wanking.'

'They grow up so fast these days,' I muse. 'As long as she washes her hands when she's finished.'

'She licks most of it off.'

'Jim, you are talking about a child, a thirteen-year-old child.'

'You make me sound like a paedophile.'

'Don't tell me—'

'Calm down, Spec. Only in my fantasies.'

'What fantasies?'

'The ones I have about your niece.'

'You are one sick giraffe.'

'Dead giraffe. Hey, look,' Jim says excitedly, 'she's got her playmate with her, Perky.'

Perky is a girl in Pinky's class at school. I can just about make them out, lit up in the ghost giraffe's resplendent glow. 'Who do those feet belong to?'

'Perky,' Jim says. 'Or is it Pinky?'

'You tell me,' I say cuttingly. 'You're the pervert.'

'I love it when they talk in those cute voices. Do you know what your niece calls her clitoris? Perky. And Perky calls hers Pinky.'

'What is it with my family? Any other revelations, Jim? I suppose we're off to Fig's room next.'

'You're not taking that thing in there,' Jim says, indicating the point in the front of my moon-coloured boxer shorts. 'You'll get us arrested.'

'You first.'

'Jim, after you.'

'I always go first.'

'Only because you're so rude.'

'Underpants,' Jim says amicably. 'Faded, with tatty elastic.'

'Well, we can't stand here all night. One of us has to go first.'

Jim shrugs. It isn't going to be him.

'Fine.' I open my youngest surviving relative's door. 'Ah, she's asleep.'

'Lift the duvet.'

'That will definitely get me arrested.'

'Only if you enjoy it,' Jim remarks. 'Lift it.'

'No.'

'Lift it, before I do.'

'Anything for a quiet life.' I fold back one of the duvet's corners. And there, in the glow of the landing light, is my nine-year-old niece. 'You see, Jim. The world isn't completely disgusting. Now, what did you want to show me?'

'Nothing.'

'Then why are we in here?'

'It was your idea, Spec.'

'Was it? Then we should leave.' I follow Jim to the door, then stop for one last look at the child. 'Oh, Jim,' I sigh, 'why can't they stay like that for ever?'

'Be riding horses in a few years, just like your wife.'

'I should never have bought her that pony. Mind you, she does adore it.'

'She doesn't adore you though, Spec.'

'What?'

'She thinks you're a poop.'

'A what?'

'Look at the blackboard.'

I do. It says: 'Uncle Scott is a poop.' In big letters. Thick, heavy letters, as though the stick of chalk was held by a hoof. 'Is this your doing?'

'Eh?'

'You wrote this, didn't you? Another of your feeble attempts at alienating me from my family.'

'Family this, family that,' Jim says scathingly. 'You're the one who keeps on about them. Well, you know what you can do with your fucking family.'

'Why, Jim,' I say, folding my arms across my Space Man T-shirt, 'I do believe you are jealous. Jealous because I am the man who has everything, and you are nothing but a gormless ghost giraffe.'

Not much he can say to that. He's in a corner, and he knows it. 'All right, I did write it. But only for a joke. I thought it would make you laugh.'

I shake my head, unconvinced. 'You really are pathetic. Not only are you jealous, but you're not even giraffe enough to admit it.'

Jim picks up one of Fig's toys, a chubby rubber man dressed in a wrestler's leotard. 'Stretch Armlong,' he says with his mouth full. 'Grab the other end.'

I hold Stretch Armlong by the legs, the head gripped firmly in the giraffe's tombstone teeth. He backs on to the landing, and I follow.

'Stay in there.'

I stand in Fig's room as Jim backs out across the landing, demonstrating why the toy is called Stretch.

'Stretch Armlong,' Jim says from the far end of the landing. 'You can get a dog, Dog Leglong.'

'She does have a birthday coming up.'

'Guess what I can do?' With me still holding the legs, Jim proceeds to perform a rather impressive manoeuvre. With a flick of his head, he has the elongated rubber human tied in a knot. 'I can do the same trick with my own neck,' he says. And he does.

'I never knew giraffes were so supple.'

'I can suck myself off, too.'

'Jim, please.'

'Are you all right, Spec? You look like you've seen a ghost.'

'Sex talk always makes me queasy.'

'Talking of sex talk,' Jim says. His voice sounds odd with that rubber head in his mouth. 'Have you ever phoned one of those sex lines?'

'You must be joking. Fifty pence a minute. A pound at peak rate.'

'You've obviously done your research. I can see your point though, Spec. With your horrible dick—'

'My dick isn't horrible.'

'Then why does your wife call it the gruesome dangler?'

'She does not. She calls it, um—' I let go of one of the toy's legs and press my thumb against my spectacles, channelling the pressure directly into my frontal memory lobe. 'It was a long time ago.'

'What was?'

'Our honeymoon. Oh, I remember. She called it my cavalier.'

'That's not what she wrote in her diary.'

'You really are one nosy giraffe. Mind you, with a nose like that—' The moment these words are out, Jim releases his teeth from Stretch Armlong's head, and the rubber toy pings me hilariously in the face. 'Ouch.'

'What other toys has she got?'

I close Fig's door. 'You're not going back in there.'

'All right, your sister's room.'

'Out of bounds,' I state firmly. 'She feels vulnerable enough as it is, with her husband in prison. And there isn't anywhere else. That was your last avenue for mischief, wasn't it. Um, wasn't it?'

Jim shakes his head, smiling his stupid clever smile.

'Where then?'

'How about my room?'

And before I can say what room, you have no room, or something like that, there is a flash of darkness and we are transported back across suburbia to my house.

'But Jim,' I say, scratching my spectacles, 'this is the utility room.'

'I know. I'm thinking of moving in.'

'Then what's stopping you?'

'It's a bit, um—'

'Yes?'

'Rubbish.'

'Jim, my utility room is not rubbish. Take a look at this,' I say, indicating a high-tech washer-dryer. With a flick of a switch, the front panel pops open to reveal a pristine pair of casual cargo trousers.

'They're grey,' Jim says.

'Exciting colour, grey,' I explain. 'Spaceships are grey, Jim.'

'Have you ever seen a spaceship then, Spec?'

'Not in real life. But I have built a model.' I reach up on

to a high shelf and lift down a proud plastic space cruiser.

'You have been a busy boy,' Jim says sarcastically. 'It's covered in spunk.'

'This isn't spunk, Jim. It's glue.'

'Then why is it oozing down the side?'

'I got a bit overexcited.'

'And you reckon I'm disgusting. What else have you got?' Jim says, rummaging. 'What's this?'

'My mobile phone.'

'Tasty.'

'Plug that back in at once,' I demand. 'It's recharging. What are you doing?'

'Stuffing it up my nose,' Jim says, stuffing it up his nose.

'Take it out.'

'It's gone all the way up. Can you reach it?'

I step on to the desk chair. 'Bend your neck.'

'Hold on, Spec. I'm going to sneeze.'

'Wait, I'll get a tissue.'

'Giraffe snot travels at nine hundred kilometres a second,' Jim says in a meanwhile-here-is-some-music sort of voice. 'Fast enough to impregnate a sperm whale.'

I dash out of the utility room, up the stairs, into the bathroom and grab a roll of toilet roll. Then, mentally comparing the width of the toilet roll with the width of the giraffe's nose, I put it down, run down the stairs to the kitchen, grab a roll of kitchen roll and dash back into the utility room.

'What's that for?'

'You said you were going to sneeze.'

'Did I?'

I consider this for a moment, then say: 'I must be having a bad night.'

'You're not the one with a mobile phone up his nose. Get up here and pull it out.'

I step on to the desk chair, up on to the desk and reach up into Jim's head. With one soggy plop, the box of tricks pops out, spraying my Space Man T-shirt with snot.

'Thanks, Spec. Remind me to do the same for you one day. Hey, is this your computer? We could download some porn.'

I shake my head. I'm looking down at my Space Man T-shirt, at the snot. 'Look,' I say, indicating the snot.

'I'm not interested,' Jim says. 'I want to look at porn.'

With an audible sigh, I switch on the computer and stand back. Numbers appear, followed by an icon of a tortoise. Then, the whole system freezes up. 'It always does this.'

'I thought you'd have top-of-the-range, what with being a geek.'

'This is top-of-the-range.'

'Oh.'

'Computers are like buses,' I say cleverly. 'You wait ages for them, then they crash.'

Jim ought to laugh at this. Instead, he gives me a look of utter, utter contempt, shakes his head and says nothing.

'Sorry. Um, where were we?'

'Trying to start your computer. Shall I perform a hardware reset?'

'If you must.'

He shoves me to one side and gives the machine a good old-fashioned hoofing. It reboots itself, and starts first time. 'Type in a word.'

'What sort of word?'

'Um. Something that excites you.'

I type in the word spaceship and press enter.

Jim looks at the screen, then turns his head sideways, and looks again. 'I didn't know you could do that.'

'Zero gravity,' I sigh. 'They might at least take their helmets off first.'

'Try something else. Close your eyes and type the first thing that comes into your head.'

I do. And, quick as a slow-motion flash, the screen fills with a high-resolution image of a woman, rolling naked on a bed, sucking her big toe.

Jim awakes me with the kiss of life.

'Stop that,' I splutter. 'No tongues.' His head seems to shrink as he straightens his neck, his ears brushing the ceiling. 'Just help me up.'

'Congratulations,' Jim says, offering me a hoof. 'You have just discovered your fetish.'

'My what?'

'Your fetish, Spec. Your thing.'

'What thing?'

'The feet porn gave you a stiffy. The blood rushed to your boxer shorts, and you passed out.'

'Nonsense.'

'Rise, sole sniffer.'

'What did you just call me?'

'On second thoughts,' Jim says, kicking me back to the carpet, 'kneel, slave, and worship my mighty hoofs.'

'Get that cloven great thing away from my face,' I scold. 'You might have trodden in something. Jim, I want to make this absolutely clear. I, Scott Spectrum, do not have a foot fetish.'

'Prove it.'

'Fine,' I say confidently. 'How?'

'Follow me.'

'Where to?'

'To see your wife,' Jim says, floating up through the ceiling.

I, being a mere mortal, have no choice but to take the stairs. 'What has this got to do with my wife?' I enquire, switching on the bedside lamp.

'She's got feet, hasn't she? Roll back the duvet.'

'She might wake up.'

'I'll do one of my big rippers,' Jim says, pointing his hindquarters at my wife's head.

'We want to sedate her, not kill her.'

'Just get on with it.'

I stand at the foot of the bed and roll back the duvet. And here are my wife's feet, naked as the day they were born, attached, one each, to each of her two ankles.

'Go on, Spec. Have a sniff.'

'The only thing I can smell, Jim Giraffe, is your spectral bum.'

He wags his paintbrush tail, painting the room with fresh air. 'That should do it.'

'Here goes nothing.' I choose a foot, part two toes, and inhale.

'With your clothes off.'

'Just my top then,' I say, slipping out of my Space Man T-shirt.

'And the rest.'

I sigh loudly, shake my head, mutter something futile and step out of my shorts. As I slip the big toe between my lips, Jim vanishes and my wife sits up. 'Scott, what are you doing?'

'Continence,' I say, wondering what to say. 'Um. I just had the strangest dream.'

She moves her brown hair from her eyes. 'What sort of dream?'

'I dreamt I was a baby, sucking your thumb.'

'My thumb?'

'Mine was too small. I was a baby, you see.'

'Scott,' she says, folding her arms across the bumpy area of her nightie, 'are you making this up?'

'No. Well, yes.'

She moves her brown hair back into her eyes. 'You silly thing. Come back to bed. If you wanted to suck my toes, you only had to ask.'

I smile. 'Really?'

'Yes, really. Now come back to bed.'

I stand up, inadvertently revealing the full extent of my nudity.

Continence looks at my middle, and smiles. 'It's nice to see your cavalier for a change.'

Before I can say, 'Oh dear my boxer shorts must have fallen off,' or something like that, my chest is gripped by a cake-shaped pain and I fall to the carpet, clutching the affected area.

'If you would have a wank once in a while,' Continence says, 'these things wouldn't happen.'

Hold on—

That isn't Continence. It's Jim, sat up in my wife's bed, wearing her nightie. 'Jim, what have you done with my wife?'

'She popped out for emergency medical supplies,' Jim says, casually picking up a magazine.

'Who put me to bed? What time is it?' The curtains are still drawn across the window, but the morning sunlight is bright enough to light up the whole room. I hold a hand to my heart, and count the beats. One. Two. And then it misses one. 'This is real, isn't it?'

'As real as I am.'

'But can it really be cured by masturbation?'

'More or less,' Jim says, casually turning the page.

I get out of bed. 'Right, where do I start?'

'Eh?'

'I need you to talk me through it.'

Jim wrinkles his nose. 'Grab those tissues.'

I take the box of tissues from the dresser and spread some over the carpet, taking care not to leave any gaps.

'Now take your clothes off, and get on with it.'

'Look away then.'

'I need to keep an eye on you, Spec. You might pull it off.'

'I thought that was the idea.'

As is usually the case when I tell a joke, rather than laugh, the ghost giraffe merely looks at me with disdain. He does this to annoy me. Ironically, the moment I remove my moon-coloured boxer shorts he lets out an hysterical hoot. By the time I start work on my penis, he's rolling about on the floor, slapping his ghostly thigh.

'Jim, you're making me feel terribly self-conscious.' I close my eyes and try to imagine my wife, running barefoot on a deserted beach. As my penis grows, Jim grows too, till all I see are testicles, two yellow-blue pendulums that swing before my eyes and knock me for six. 'Jim,' I cry, 'you're huge!'

And suddenly, it is all over and my life reverts to comedy.

'Get your phantom genitals out of my face.'

'Sorry, it's just my way.'

'Talk about over-friendly.' I bend down to pull up my boxer

shorts, and discover that I have accidentally overshot the tissues.

'Oh hell,' I exclaim. 'I got some on my wife's mail-order clothing catalogue.'

'Right, well, I'll be off then.'

'Jim,' I exclaim, 'what am I going to do?'

'Don't ask me, Spec. I have a bus to catch.'

'But Jim—'

I tear out the page and screw it into a sperm-filled ball. Running to the bathroom, I lift the toilet seat and flush it into the land of poo and pee. 'You giraffes are nothing but trouble,' I yell, waving my fist at the see-through usurper. 'Get out of my sight. Before I call the police.'

Cops R Tops

Continence and I are watching television. Or trying to, but the man next door is also watching television, and his long-range aerial is interfering with our picture. For several minutes, I try to ignore it. Then, I stand up, clear my throat, open my mouth to speak, close it again and sit back down.

Continence smoothes down her long brown hair. 'Don't let it upset you. There isn't even anything on.'

'I keep trying to get into this police drama.'

'But Scott, you're not even looking at the screen.'

'I have to check this script,' I say, holding up a pile of white typed pages. 'Space Man In Space. Episode one, series three.'

'Then tell me what is happening.'

'Well, Space Man is in space, and—'

'I meant on the television.'

I point at one of the police officers. 'Something to do with that man there. He's running after someone. Or away from someone. Either way, he's running.'

'He's very fast.'

'You would have to be,' I say authoritatively, 'to be in the police force.'

'Look, he's pulled out a gun.'

'Damn,' I exclaim as the picture fuzzes up. 'Just when it was getting exciting. I can't see a thing, can you?'

'Only the soles of his shoes. There, at the bottom of the screen. And there's the top of his hat.'

'Now what's happened? The whole picture has flipped upside down.'

'No, Scott. He's dropped his hat, and he's fallen over a wall and got his legs caught up in a tree.'

'Shall I give it a hoof? I mean a kick. If this keeps up,' I threaten, 'I'm going to go round there and say something.'

'You need to keep calm, Scott. We don't want you to start seeing that talking zebra again.'

'He isn't a zebra, he's a giraffe. And he's real. Unfortunately. Right, that's it,' I say, as the screen fuzzes up again, 'I'm going round there.' I stand from my high-tech armchair, pause just long enough for my wife to stop me doing anything I might regret, then sit back down.

'I thought you were going round there.'

'The picture is fine now. I can see his beer belly.'

'It's supposed to be a rippling torso,' Continence explains. 'The picture has gone all squashed. Perhaps you should go round there. Be careful though, Scott. He is bigger than you.'

Bigger, yes. But, I ask myself, does bigger mean better? I consider how my penis compares with my wife's dildo, and conclude that, yes, it does. 'Right,' I say, standing up. 'Nobody spoils Scott Spectrum's weekend viewing.' And I'm out the front door without even putting on my trainers.

Rat-a-tat-tat goes the knocker, as my heart goes thump thump thump. And before my brain can ask my body what on earth it thinks it is doing, the front door opens and I'm greeted by our next-door neighbour, Eddy.

'Eddy,' I say, looking up at the underside of his chin. 'Uh, how are you?'

'Watching a bit of telly. That police drama, Cops R Tops. Pick it up on the long-range.'

'Funny, we can get it on the short-range.'

'These are new ones, Scott. Much better than the old ones. The old ones are shit.'

'Eddy, your aerial is interfering with our picture. I want you to go in there—' But even as I speak, a ring donut squeezes my windpipe and I'm all caked out.

And here I am, flat out on Eddy's garden path. My wife is here, loosening the collar of my Space Man In Space special edition shirt, as Eddy straightens my spectacles and the elderly lady from across the road removes my alien-shaped slippers. Everything looks odd, as though viewed through a lens. Me, my wife, our neighbour Eddy, and the elderly lady, Granny Bagpuss. And towering above is ol' Treetops Breath, Jim Giraffe, his stupid face lit by a huge yellow-blue grin.

'Jim, I've had my second heart attack.'

'So what do you want, a medal?'

'A bit of sympathy would be nice.'

Jim contorts his neck until his face meets mine, and with

breath as fresh as leaves from the very tops of the trees, he says: 'Bollocks.'

'Come on, Jim. Show some compassion.'

'Some what?'

'I thought we were finished with all this. I masturbated three times last week, once to completion. I even bought a specialist foot-fetish magazine, Sniffer.'

'Pull yourself together, Spec. Pucker up, and give your wife a big tonsil snog.'

'Anything,' I plead, 'just give me another chance.'

'It's not up to me. I'm just the messenger. Now snap out of it, before that old dear runs off with your slippers.'

'Scott,' my wife says as I sit up, 'we thought we'd lost you.'

'We thought you'd kicked the bucket,' Eddy says.

'My alien-shaped slippers,' I cry. 'Where are my alien-shaped slippers?'

All eyes turn to Granny Bagpuss, who has slipped them on over her own slippers and waddled off across the road.

I stand up, brush myself down. 'Continence, it is time for a new me.' I step forward and plant a deep, passionate kiss on her forehead, then turn to my neighbour. 'Eddy, I think your long-range television aerial is terrific.'

'Do you want to come and watch my telly?'

'Um—'

'In you come,' Eddy says, ushering me into the house. 'Up the apples and pears.'

Now, I may not be working class, but I can tell from the context that Eddy is inviting me up to his bedroom. And, what with me being the new me, I have no choice but to accept. I wave goodbye to Continence— who takes her hand from the pocket of her long brown skirt to wave back— and walk in through Eddy's front door, closing it behind me. 'Is your wife home?'

'She moved out, Scott. No time for her. Too much on the telly.'

'What a pity.'

'Life is terminally tragic,' Eddy says, quoting a passage from Cops R Tops. 'Up and down the apples and pears we go, and for what. When all we have to live for. Is arresting people. And kicking them in the head.'

'Indeed.'

'You know who said that, don't you, Scott?'

'Inspector Blue?'

'Inspector Black,' Eddy says. 'Inspector Blue is the one with the bad temper.'

'It wasn't apples and pears though, was it, Eddy? It was the high street. Up and down the high street we go, and for what.'

Eddy looks at me like I'm an idiot. 'The way I see it, Scott, is this. Everything, right, is shit.'

'And?'

'And what?'

'Oh.'

Eddy stops midway across the landing. 'Have a butcher's around you, and tell me one thing you see that isn't shit.'

He does have a point. Like all working-class people, Eddy has no money, and any money he does have is spent on lottery tickets, alcohol, cigarettes, tabloid newspapers and soft porn. 'It seems to me, Eddy, that you could do with a holiday.'

Eddy shakes his head. 'Too cold.'

'You could go somewhere hot.'

'Too hot,' he says, leading me into the bedroom. 'Better off where I am.'

I nod.

'You're a funny bloke, Scott. First you have a moan about my aerial messing up your telly, then you come round and watch mine.'

And on seeing the interior of Eddy's bedroom, I begin to wish that I hadn't bothered. One half of the double bed is piled high with a jumble of coloured wires, leaving just enough space for Eddy. In the window, a halo of daylight gathers round a widescreen television, noisily sporting a beard of chaotic blue fuzz.

Eddy passes me a remote control. 'Use this to move the effing aerial.'

The aerial is huge, bigger than a car, a hatchback, or possibly an estate. As I fiddle with the remote control, I hear it leaping about above, as the screen fills with a multitude of images. A cowboy trying on a new pair of trousers, sumo lap dancing and animals performing magic tricks. 'The picture quality is not as I had expected.'

'Interference.'

'From what?'

'Your effing telly.'

'Never. You should have told us. We would have switched it off.'

'That wouldn't be neighbourly.'

'I suppose not,' I say, blushing in shame. 'Eddy, I have an idea. As you may know, I work in television. Some of my colleagues are currently testing a new prototype television aerial, the tallest ever built. I can have them install it out there, in your back garden.'

'Out there? In my back garden?'

I nod.

'Effing hell,' Eddy says, with eyeballs the size of footballs. 'Maybe everything isn't shit after all.'

Three days later, Eddy and I are in Eddy's back garden, gazing up at the new aerial. With its length and thickness, its cable veins and domed tip, it reminds me of something. Though I cannot think what.

'Speechless. Effing speechless.'

'Me too,' I say, also speechless.

'If only my wife was here.'

'Why, do you think she would be impressed?'

'No,' he says, 'I'm just wondering who's going to clean it.'

'Married life didn't suit you, did it, Eddy?'

'The way I look at it, is that marriage is shit.'

'I like being married,' I say, smiling over the fence at my wife. She lifts her hand from the pocket of her long brown skirt to wave back. 'Continence and I are as happy as pie.'

'Shit pie.'

'Not at all,' I say in the pie's defence. 'Blackberry and apple. With a generous sprinkling of sugar.'

'Sugar is bad for your teeth,' Eddy says, baring his bad teeth. 'See those blokes over there.' He indicates the team of electrical installers on the patio, enjoying a well-earned cup of tea. 'Did you see how much sugar they had in their tea? Five lumps each. Mind you, they know how to install an aerial.'

One of the electrical installers wipes his concrete-encrusted boots on the grass and wanders over. 'One thousand tons of steel. Fifty metres tall, ten metres diameter. And we installed it.'

'Effing right,' Eddy says. 'Can we switch it on?'

The electrical installer shakes his head. 'Not fully tested. Have the whole street up in smoke. Right, come on, lads.'

As they gather up their tool kits, a shadow falls over them, eerie and blue. Being working-class stereotypes, they do not see it, and neither of course does Eddy, but I do, and I recognise its antecedent as Jim. Ever the competitor, the ghost giraffe has grown to the size of the aerial, which he now proceeds to mount. 'Jim, get down from there,' I shout. 'It isn't fully tested.'

'What do you think I'm doing now?' Jim says, humping for all he is worth. 'If it survives this, it'll survive anything.'

'I do hope you're wearing a condom.'

'Bollocks.'

'Why must you use words as a defence mechanism? You wear language like a verbal suit of armour.'

'Hold on,' Jim says, 'let me just shoot my load.' He does so, filling the aerial with a thick, creamy mist. 'Now, where were we?'

'You tell me.'

'I know,' he says, shrinking to a more manageable size, 'I was about to call you a prat. For planting a giant heap of scrap metal in your neighbour's back garden.'

'You didn't seem to mind it a moment ago.'

'It's a good shag, Spec, but I wouldn't want to marry it. I might get brain cancer.'

'Jim, television aerials do not cause brain cancer.'

'You're living next door to the biggest radiation hotspot in all suburbia. You might just as well rent a penthouse at a nuclear power station.'

'But it brings so much joy. Just look at the look on Eddy's face.'

He does.

I do, too.

'He's nuts,' Jim says.

'Pardon?'

'He's nuts.'

I take another look. He does look nuts. 'Maybe he's in a state of shock.'

'Well, who wouldn't be,' Jim says, scratching the inside of his nose. 'He's got a phallus outside his kitchen window.'

'Jim, that is not a phallus.'

'It's a phallus. A massive metal cock. All that reverse psychology stuff is bollocks. It's a cock, and you erected it because you were too pathetic to stand up to Eddy.'

'Unfounded.'

'This aerial, Spec, is an extension of your penis. A sword for your so-called cavalier. It may be in Eddy's back garden, but it's you who had it installed and everybody knows it.'

'It was a gift for Eddy,' I say weakly. 'To enhance the picture on his television.'

'This isn't about television, Spec. It's about how big you feel when your wife looks over the garden fence. Because let's face it, like everything else in this world, it all boils down to cock. How big it is and where you stick it.'

I pause for a moment, while I formulate my defence. Or should that be attack. Either way, I pause for a moment to formulate it, then go in for the kill. 'Such cynicism, from one so long-necked. I can tell you spent your formative years in the jungle. Running from cheetahs and the like.'

'Running from cheetahs? I used to step over them. They'd stop in their tracks and scratch their soppy ears and say: Where did he go? Then, I would lower my head and my upside-down face would come into view and they would leap out of their spots. And I would hold up my head and stride off.'

'Nonsense. No giraffe ever walked away from a big cat.

Not after making a fool of it. It would chew the meat from your ankles.'

'We giraffes don't have meat on our ankles,' Jim explains, 'for that very reason. Where was I? Yes, I would stride off into the trees, with the big cats looking at me thinking: There he goes. The true king of the jungle.'

'Since when were giraffes the king of the jungle?'

'Since we were the tallest.'

'Arrogant mammal,' I mutter to myself. 'Jim, when will you learn that size does not matter?'

'Everything matters in the jungle, Spec. It's a question of survival.'

'And you would know all about that, wouldn't you. What with being dead.'

Jim says nothing to this. Not much he can say. He just stands there, looking down at the crazy paving, no doubt wishing it would open up and swallow him.

'There,' I gloat, 'that knocked you down a peg or two.'

'I advise you to shut your mouth. Before I shut it for you.'

'At least I'm alive,' I say, and skip around the garden to prove it. 'Incidentally, what did finish you off? And don't give me that nonsense about heart failure.'

'I don't like to talk about it, Spec. It puts me in a bad mood.'

'You're always in a bad mood.'

'Do you want to hear it, or not?'

'If you can open your mouth without fibbing.'

'Then if you've finished prancing about, I will begin.'

And he does.

'It all started when I heard this bang. I look round and there's this bloke with one of those guns with the funnel at the end. He'd just shot an elephant, and now he was firing at me. Fortunately, I was brought up in the toughest part of the jungle, the east side, and at the first sign of trouble my legs are trained to trot on the spot.' As he says this, he performs a fiddly jig, as though knitting an intricate garment. A pair of mittens, perhaps, or a hat.

'I thought you were going to tell me how you died.'

'That bit comes next. So I give him one of my stares, and he freezes, caught in the headlights. It was like my poker face, but with daggers.'

'I don't believe a word of this, but go on.'

'He drops his gun and scarpers. So I trample it into the dirt, and animals emerge from every corner of the jungle, and pronounce me king of the beers.'

'King of the what?'

'Beers. Due to my high alcohol tolerance.'

'But what happened to the hunter?'

'He wet himself and ran off. Then, a week later, he turns up with a whole army. Charge, they yell, that sort of caper. And here they come, on horseback mostly, but some of them had early flying machines, what you would now call aeroplanes.'

'When is all this supposed to have happened?'

'Um, two hundred years ago.'

I laugh. 'Nobody had flying machines back then.'

'Well, when I say flying machines, they were more like hopping machines,' Jim says, peddling backwards. 'Spindly wooden things, with wooden wheels.'

'The history books tell a different story.'

'Anyway, you can guess what happened next.'

'Do you know, Jim, I don't think I can.'

'Not even a giraffe can take on an entire army. Not on an empty stomach. So I popped out for fish and chips.'

'And?'

'I choked on a fish bone.'

'Oh, bad luck.'

'Everyone has to go some time. Talking of which,' Jim says. And he vanishes into the ether, the sentence left hanging, like a coat hanger.

Eddy hands me one end of a length of thick black cable. 'Take this upstairs and plug it in. I want to hug the aerial as it picks up its first show.'

'But you won't be able to see the screen.'

'Give me a shout,' Eddy says, 'when the credits have rolled.'

So I drag the cable through the house and up to Eddy's bedroom, where who should I find but Jim Giraffe. 'Not you again.'

'I haven't seen you for ages.'

'Then who was that on the patio, telling tall tales?'

'You tell me. Was he tall? Did he have a tail?'

This time it is my turn to stare blankly.

'Fair enough. What do you want to watch?'

'We have to get it working first. What do I do with this?'

'Read the instruction manual,' Jim says, lifting his hoof from a white printed booklet.

I bend down and pick it up. 'Connecting your new proto- type television aerial to your television,' I read. 'Step one. Locate the long black cable. It should have two ends. One at each end.'

'Give it to me.'

'Don't you get teeth marks in that.'

He drops his head behind the television and plugs it in. The cable, not his head. Though it might as well be his head.

I take the remote control, step out on to the landing, point the remote control through the doorway and press a button. Jim, stood in front of the telly, his nose practically touching the screen, doesn't bat an eyelid. Either he has shrunk, or the television has grown to an unprecedented size. As you might expect, the screen is filled with fuzz, but it has to be the most extraordinary fuzz you could ever see.

'That aerial,' Jim explains, tuning it in, 'is so powerful, it can pick up programmes that haven't even been made yet.'

'Such as.'

'Space Man In Space. Episode three, series ten.'

It starts— as always— with Space Man floating through space, but he is wearing a new spacesuit, and the pattern of stars is more complex, with galaxies opening out to reveal new galaxies within. We have even messed with the theme tune. It's still got that catchy da, da da da, da da dada daa, but the arrangement is different, with more oomph. The name of the show appears, Space Man In Space, in heavy monolithic type, emerging from a black hole and spinning out of control. And being eaten by a space monster. To be perfectly honest, the whole thing is a bit tacky.

Having joined the series halfway through, I'm not sure what is going on, but Space Man appears to be on board a space station, tucked up in a space bunk. The lighting is set to rest-and-recuperation levels, his space helmet is at the foot of the bunk and no doubt his spacesuit is hanging up in the anti-static storage chamber.

Ever on the alert, Space Man is wide awake, holding the bubble-wrap space duvet tight against his chest, presumably for warmth. But there is an odd look on his face. It looks like fear, which seems unlikely as Space Man has always been fearless. Suddenly, the door to the anti-static storage chamber slides open and out steps some kind of space creature. Tall, green, long-necked, with four legs and suckers for feet. And what is that on his head? It looks like a pair of space-regulation underpants. 'Greetings,' he says. 'My name is Jimp, and I am a space goraf, from the planet Jumple.'

Space Man pulls the bubble-wrap space duvet up to his chin. 'Don't kill me,' he pleads, quite out of character. 'Please don't kill me.'

The space goraf paces the room for a bit, then stops at the side of the bunk and says: 'Do not be alarmed, for I mean you no harm. Um, do you have any space beer?'

'In— in the space fridge,' Space Man stammers, pointing at the space fridge.

Jimp kicks open the space-fridge door, bites the cap from a bottle of space beer, downs the contents in one, belches, and says: 'I have to go now. But I will return.' He steps back into the anti-static storage chamber, the door sliding closed behind him.

In the next scene, Space Man is in the space-station canteen, drinking a mug of cocoa. His hand shakes so violently that the cocoa spills down his regulation space vest. The space-station captain, in full space-station regalia, looks across the table at Space Man and says: 'Space Man, I want to see you in my office. Right after lunch.'

Space Man watches the captain eat his space pudding, then follows him down the corridor and through a sliding space door to the captain's space desk.

'Space Man, you are an insult to the space station. We are under attack from intergalactic robots and there you are spilling your cocoa. Now, what have you got to say for yourself?'

'It— it was in the storage chamber.'

The captain seats himself behind the desk. He indicates for Space Man to sit down, but Space Man can only stare wide-eyed, opening and closing his mouth. 'Speak,' the captain yells, 'or I shall have you expelled from the academy.'

Space Man holds up his hand to indicate something a good deal taller than himself. 'Tall,' he manages. 'Alien.'

With an authoritative sigh, the captain presses a button on his desk and speaks into a concealed microphone. 'Security, we have a code three zero five.'

Two security guards burst in, grab Space Man by the arms and march him off to a padded cell.

The camera closes in on Space Man's face. As it pulls back, the lighting changes to indicate that time has passed, and a space-goraf-shaped shadow appears, stretching across the padded floor. 'Greetings,' Jimp says. 'I have returned. Now that you are out of the way, it is time for me to kill all the robots.'

There then follow several scenes in which the space goraf flies around the space station, kicking intergalactic robots in the head and tearing off their bendy robotic arms.

I switch off the set. 'This is just a vehicle for your new acting career, isn't it.'

'I don't know what you mean.'

'I can picture it now. You, sat in Harry Maker's office, your hoofs up on his desk, charming his knickers off with tales of your exploits back in the jungle. Yes, you learnt acting back in the jungle, outwitting a lion.'

'Bollocks.'

'He's so taken in, he draws up a contract there and then, and the next thing you know, you're stretched out in a jacuzzi, naked girls lathering your flank.'

'Bollocks,' he says again, but this time he's grinning.

'Why do you have to spoil things? Why can't you just leave me alone?'

Jim laughs. He stretches out his legs, he's back in Harry Maker's office, smoking an imaginary cigar. Well, I say back, but I should say forward, as none of this has happened yet.

'It's all a big joke to you. Jim, this is my career, my livelihood. What happens when the show bombs, what happens then? We have a highly devoted fan base. The average Space Man fan knows the Space Man character inside out. You can't put him in a loony bin,' I claim, 'he'd be out of there in a second.'

'Not if he's lost his edge.'

'Who wrote that nonsense anyway? The dialogue is spot on, I admit that, but the characterisation is all over the place. I would never write it like that.'

'It isn't you who writes it,' Jim explains. 'They bring in a new team of writers. Harry Maker wants to phase out the Space Man character completely.'

I open my mouth to speak, but nothing comes out.

'Don't take it so personally, Spec. It's not as though Space Man is based on you. Or is he?'

'Well.' I sit on the edge of the space bunk. I mean, bed. 'As an artist, one inevitably puts a certain amount of oneself into one's creation. What are you laughing at? Stop laughing, or I'll hit you.'

'No wonder you get on well with Eddy', Jim says. 'You've got a violent streak, just like him.'

'Eddy hasn't got a violent streak,' I say, looking out of the window. He is still down in the back garden, his arms around the base of the aerial.

'He's a psycho. You know where his wife is, don't you. There, on the bed, under all them wires.'

I look at the bed, one side of which is piled high with a jumble of coloured wires. 'No, I saw her out in the garden just last week. I was chatting to her over the fence. She wanted me to write a computer program to predict the results of the National Lottery.'

'And you told her to fuck off.'

'I told her I would do it. I like the National Lottery, Jim. It gives ordinary people a chance to shine.'

'Stupidity tax.'

'Pardon?'

'The National Lottery is a tax on stupidity. The more stupid you are, the more you play. And the more you pay.'

'Anyhow, I agreed to write it for her, and I will.' I rub my thoughtful spectacle frames. 'Or I might ask my best friend to write it, Vic Twenty.'

'No point now. Later that day, she was up here with Eddy. She was stood just there, by that pair of odd socks.'

I look at the socks. Very odd.

'Eddy was trying to watch telly, but she wouldn't stop talking. Turn it down, she says. Why do you never talk? Shut your mouth, he says. You never stop talking. Shut your mouth and let me watch telly. But she keeps on talking. So he stands up, picks up that heap of wires and dumps it on her head.'

'Nonsense. They must weigh a ton. Not even Eddy could pick them all up, not in one go.'

'Well, it didn't happen quite like that,' Jim says, peddling backwards. 'What he did was, he picked them up one at a time and threw them at her. With every wire that struck her, her strength ebbed away, until finally she lost the will to live.'

'It would take too long. She would get up and leave the room.'

'All right. He picks up a wire and strangles her. Then,

he's got the body to dispose of. But he can't be bothered. So he buries her in wires and nips off down the pub.'

'Plausible,' I concede, 'but you've ruined any credibility your story might have had by altering it.'

'If you don't believe me, take a look.'

'No,' I say. 'I don't like to.'

'Go on.'

'I think I might go home.'

'Off you go then.'

I stand up from the bed. The problem is, the wires are on the side nearest the door, and I would have to walk past them to get to it. 'I might just stay over here.'

'Fair enough.'

Yes, I tell myself. I shall sit here and listen to the birds as they sing their suburban songs.

Not that I can hear any birds.

They have all flown away.

Or died, and dropped to the ground.

'Jim, I've got my eyes closed and I want you to guide me.'

'Where to?'

'My duvet. Via the quickest possible route. Which does not involve contact with a corpse. Jim. Jim, are you there?'

When I open my eyes, the room is lit by flashing blue police lights, and Jim is gone.

I run past the heap of coloured wires, down the stairs to the kitchen window. Eddy is walking across the garden towards me, no doubt with murderous intent. I open the back door, yell an accusation of uxoricide, slam the door in his face and draw the bolt. I run to the front door, invite the policeman inside, tell him about the body and send him upstairs.

A few minutes later, he comes back down. 'Is this some kind of joke?'

'No, officer,' I say gravely. 'Murder is no laughing matter.'

I follow him back up the stairs. He has moved the wires to the other side of the bed, revealing the flattened body that lies beneath.

Oh. It isn't Eddy's murdered wife after all, but a life-size cardboard cut-out of Inspector Blue, a character from Cops R Tops.

I look at the cardboard police officer on the bed, then up at the real police officer, not from Cops R Tops. 'The plot thickens,' I say hopefully. 'What could it all mean?'

The policeman shakes his head. 'I doubt that it means anything.'

'Then why did you come round here,' I quiz, 'if not to investigate a murder?'

'There has been a spate of thefts in the area,' he explains. 'Footwear. Of the indoor variety.'

'Slippers.'

He nods.

'Then maybe I can help you after all.'

Out in the street, Eddy comes up to me and says: 'Did you just call me a murderer and slam the door in my face?'

'Yes,' I say sheepishly. 'Sorry. I thought you were someone else.'

He nods.

The policeman taps his helmet impatiently, tap tap tap, so I wave goodbye to Eddy and lead the policeman across the road to the home of Granny Bagpuss.

She takes ages to come to the door, but, being a proper old-fashioned granny, she is worth the wait. 'Hello, officer. Would you like to come in?'

'I'm coming too,' I say, following in his imposing footsteps.

Granny Bagpuss closes the door and shows us into the lounge. 'Would you like a cup of tea? You can have one each. I have plenty of cups.'

The policeman and I sit on the sofa, me at one end, the policeman at the other. I try to think of something to say, but then Granny Bagpuss comes back and hands us each a cup. The tea is cold, but we don't say anything, as Granny Bagpuss is old.

'Mrs Bagpuss,' the policeman says, 'would you mind if I ask you a personal question? How many pairs of slippers do you own?'

'About thirty.'

'Thirty.'

'Yes,' she says, stirring her tea.

'And how many feet do you have?'

'How many feet? Or pairs of feet?'

The policeman looks at me, clearly out of his depth. 'Do the whole thing in pairs,' I tell him. 'It's easier for comparison.'

'Pairs of feet.'

Granny Bagpuss thinks for a moment, scanning the question for tricks, then says: 'One pair.'

'Then is there any particular reason why you would own thirty pairs of slippers?'

She frowns. 'I don't wear them all at once, if that's what you mean.'

'Mrs Bagpuss, am I correct in assuming that you survive on the state pension?'

'I do, yes.'

'Measured in pairs of slippers, how much is the state pension, would you say, Mrs Bagpuss?'

She thinks for a moment, then says that she isn't sure.

I raise my hand. 'May I answer that?'

The policeman nods.

'With one week's pension, you would get two pairs of slippers, three if you bought them on the market.'

'Mrs Bagpuss, I am arresting you on suspicion of footwear theft. You do not have to say anything, but anything you do say will be held against you, particularly if it involves slippers.'

'Talking of slippers,' I say as the policeman fastens the cuffs, 'can I have my slippers back?'

The policeman shakes his head. 'All slippers on these premises will be taken in for analysis by our team of forensic experts.'

'Granny Bagpuss,' I say, thinking fast, 'may I use your toilet?'

'As long as you don't leave the seat up.'

I walk out of the room, as casual as can be, then run up the stairs and into Granny Bagpuss's bedroom. I open the wardrobe door, and thirty pairs of slippers fall out, followed by ol' Treetops Breath, Jim Giraffe. 'Oh,' he says. 'Hello.'

'What are you doing here?'

'I might just as well ask you the same question.'

'You're the one hiding in an elderly lady's wardrobe.'

'I'm a ghost giraffe,' Jim says, by way of explanation.

'Well, I am here on official police business. Two of these slippers are mine. Though how I am going to find them I do not know, let alone match them up.'

'Here's one,' Jim says, indicating a slipper with one front hoof, 'and the other one is over there,' he says, indicating the other with the other.

'How did you do that?'

'They're shaped like space aliens,' he explains. 'All the others are plain brown, or tartan.'

I nod.

'Anyway, they smell.'

'You must have a very sensitive nose, if it can differentiate the odours of thirty pairs of slippers.' I pause for effect, then add: 'Or maybe it is just big.'

'Bollocks.'

Neither of us says anything for a bit. I pick up my alien-shaped slippers in a matter-of-fact sort of way and say: 'May I go now?'

'Don't ask me, Spec. Just because I'm ugly, it doesn't mean I'm your mother.'

'Well, if you're going to keep following me—'

'I don't keep following you.'

'Everywhere I go, you're there.'

'Then it is you who is following me. Common sense.'

'Common sense my spectacles,' I say, adjusting my spectacles. 'You're a ghost giraffe, ghost giraffes don't do common sense. Everyone knows that. Now get back in the wardrobe where you belong.'

'Fine.' He climbs back into the wardrobe. 'See you in prison, arsehole.'

I place my alien-shaped slippers over my hands, like alien-shaped gloves, and close the wardrobe door, leaving the other twenty-nine pairs scattered across the floor. I'm halfway across the room when I realise what Jim just said. 'Did you say that you would see me in prison?'

'I can't hear you,' Jim says. 'I'm in the wardrobe.'

I open the wardrobe door and ask him again.

'I might have.'

'Well, why would you say that?'

'That policeman is still downstairs,' he explains, scratching his hindquarters with the tip of his tail. 'If he sees you with those slippers, he'll arrest you for perverting the corset of justice.'

'The course of justice.'

'Perverts in corsets,' Jim says defiantly. 'The slippers need to be analysed by the science pigs.'

'There's twenty-nine pairs there. Approximately. The authorities won't miss the one pair.'

'All right, Spec, consider this. The old lady is innocent. The slippers were planted by a granny-hating maniac. A nephew with a grudge. Just one of those slippers contains a strand of the villain's ankle hair. What if that slipper is one of yours? The old lady goes down for a very long time. For a crime she didn't commit. And all because of your cosy feet.'

I bite my lip.

'Personally, I couldn't give a toss. One less slow person clogging up the supermarket. It's you I'm thinking of, Spec. Your guilty conscience.'

I smile warmly. 'Do you really mean that?'

'What?'

'What you just said. About thinking of me.'

'Don't get soppy. Not when we're alone together, in the bedroom. People will talk.'

I sit on the edge of the bed. 'But nobody knows we're here.'

'Spec, you're scaring me. You better get going, if you don't want that policeman calling for back-up.'

'I forgot about him. Goodbye, Jim.'

'Ciao.' And with a seductive rump wiggle, he disappears back among the coats.

I run back to the lounge, then, remembering the alien-shaped slippers on my hands, run back upstairs, open a window, throw them out across the back garden, and return to the lounge. 'Sorry I took so long, officer. It was a surprisingly comfortable toilet.'

The policeman and Granny Bagpuss are still sat on the sofa. Granny Bagpuss has two black eyes, something I hadn't noticed before.

'Right,' the policeman says. He stands up. Granny Bagpuss stands up too, her handcuffs rattling in the indoor breeze. Either a window is open, or one of us has a very wintry soul.

Golden Showers

Continence and I have been diagnosed brain-cancer positive. Too much watching television, Doctor Apple said. More likely it was caused by Eddy's television aerial. Either way, we have brain cancer, and we are going to die.

'Are we really going to die?' I ask him on our next visit.

My wife is sat beside me, her straight brown hair tied back in a straight brown shape, tied with a round brown hair-tie. She takes her hand from the pocket of her long brown skirt to hold my hand.

'No,' Doctor Apple says. 'We can operate. We open up the head and operate on the brain.'

I look at my wife and smile. She looks at me, not smiling. Then, she does smile. 'Doctor Apple, can you do my wife and I at the same time? We could hold hands.'

'Yes, of course.'

'How long do we have to wait?'

Doctor Apple folds back the sleeve of his shirt and looks at his watch. 'About ten minutes.'

'Well,' I say, standing up, 'we should get going.'

'We can get the bus,' Continence suggests.

'No need,' Doctor Apple says, reaching for the telephone. 'I shall order a taxi. And don't worry about the cost. It's on us.'

Continence and I exchange looks.

A few minutes later, we exchange looks again, but this time out in the surgery car park, in the sun, as the taxi pulls up at the kerb. The driver is wearing white gloves.

We hold hands throughout the entire duration of the journey. The hospital is only five minutes from the surgery, but when you are brain-cancer positive, five minutes is a long time.

The symptoms of brain cancer are difficult to describe. Continence says it is like having a grazed knee, but in your brain. You find yourself forgetting things, and remembering things. You become easily confused. You might be looking at yourself in the mirror wondering how you became so pretty, when you suddenly realise that you are actually looking at your wife.

My wife is looking out of the window. I put my hand on her shoulder and ask her if she is worried. She shakes her head.

'I am. I don't like having my head opened up. I open it up all the time, metaphorically speaking, what with being an artist. But this is different.'

She nods.

'I wonder if they remove the whole top of the head, or just open part of it, like a door.'

'They don't actually open up your head,' Continence explains. 'Doctor Apple was joking.'

'Well, it wasn't very funny.'

'Oh, Scott, he was only having a laugh.'

'Yes, but at whose expense? Talking of expense,' I say, brightening, 'wasn't it nice of the health service to pay for the taxi?'

Continence nods.

'And rightly so. We pay our taxes, they pay for our taxi.' I wait for Continence to laugh. When she doesn't, I say: 'That wasn't a pun, by the way.'

'I know,' she says, squeezing my hand.

'You would know if I had cracked a joke. Everyone would be falling about laughing. The driver would have to pull over, and we would sit in the lay-by and have a good chuckle.'

Continence smiles. I may not be able to make her laugh, but I do know how to make her smile.

This is the inside of the hospital. It looks like the outside, but inside out. There are potted trees and the walls are painted sky blue. The pillows and bedsheets are white. Continence and I are sat up in bed, holding hands. We have a room to ourselves, and they have put us in a double bed, not realising that we are a modern couple who always sleep apart. 'This is nice,' Continence says, smoothing the bedsheets. 'Sharing a bed, I mean.'

'Yes. Not very practical though.'

'How do you mean?'

I try to think of an example. 'Well, you might be asleep, and I might roll over to scratch an elbow, or a knee. That elbow or knee might poke you.'

'I wouldn't mind that.'

'It might be dangerous,' I say with very real concern. 'My knees are knobbly, and my elbows are sharp.'

'I wouldn't mind, even so.'

'But Continence, I never want to do anything to hurt you.'

She raises one of her brown eyebrows. 'Not even if I ask you to?'

'I assume you are talking theoretically.'

She looks away. 'Some things that hurt are nice.'

'Such as?'

Continence thinks for a moment, then says: 'Do you remember the time I had a bee sting on my bottom? I asked you to slap my bottom, to stop it hurting. And you did.'

'That was a strange bee sting,' I say, thinking back. 'There wasn't even a mark. Come to think of it, there wasn't even a bee.'

She smiles.

'I don't understand.'

'There was no bee sting. I made it up, so that you would slap me.'

'Continence,' I exclaim, visibly shocked.

'I hated lying to you,' she goes on, 'but it was the only way that I could make you do it. I thought to myself, how do you get a practical person to do something? You give him a practical reason.'

I nod.

'Do you remember what you said in the taxi, about being an artist? Do you really see yourself as an artist?'

I sigh a patronising sigh. 'There are two types of artist, Continence. The first type includes the poet, or the painter, or the painter and decorator. No, the painter and decorator is the second type. The second type is more practical, and produces a more practical type of art.'

'Like your Space Man In Space television show.'

'Yes. A spaceman, in space. What could be more practical than that?'

The door opens and a man walks in, holding a clipboard. 'Mr and Mrs Spectrum?'

We nod.

'I would like to introduce you to the team who will be taking care of you during your stay.' As he says this, several other people enter the room. 'This is Nurse Matron. She will be responsible for your general well-being. Taking your temperature, hugging you, that sort of thing.'

Nurse Matron steps forward. She is a big woman, but big in a nice way, like a big cake. 'Hello, Mr and Mrs Spectrum.'

'This is Professor Smarter,' the man with the clipboard says. 'Professor Smarter is head of research at Brain Cancer Research.'

Professor Smarter takes his hand out of his beige trouser pocket and holds it out for us both to shake. He is thinner than almost anybody, and has a thin beige beard. 'Hello, Scott, Continence. How lovely to meet you.'

'This is Doctor Mann,' the man with the clipboard says. 'Doctor Mann will be overlooking your case.'

Doctor Mann is a lady doctor, and is very ladylike, despite being dressed like a man. It is funny how an attractive woman can dress in men's clothing and not get laughed at or beaten up, but a man in women's clothing just looks ridiculous.

'And this is Doctor Giraffe, who will be dealing with any sexual matters.'

'Hello,' Continence says, blushing bright red.

The man with the clipboard tucks the clipboard under his arm. 'My office is just along the corridor, so if you have any problems, do give me a knock.'

'Thank you,' I say. 'It's nice to know we are in capable hands.'

'Talking of hands,' Continence says after they have all left, 'did you notice that last doctor, Doctor Giraffe? Did you notice his hands?'

'No, why?'

'They were huge,' Continence says. 'And strange.'

'I didn't notice.'

'How could you not have noticed?'

'There was a lot to take in. All these new faces. And the brain cancer is giving me a headache.'

The next day, Nurse Matron wakes us up at half past eleven. She draws the curtains, filling the room with sun. 'And how are we both today?'

'Fine,' Continence says, straightening her long brown nightie.

'I couldn't get to sleep, so I used the old wall-of-pillows trick,' I say, dismantling the wall. 'Works every time.'

'Let me administer another hug,' Nurse Matron says, pulling me from the bed and holding me. 'Your turn, Mrs Spectrum,' she says, giving my wife the same treatment.

I raise my hand. 'Nurse Matron, may I ask you a question?'

'As long as it is directly related to care work,' Nurse Matron says, straightening my spectacles.

'It sort of is.' I take a deep breath. 'Is your surname Matron, or is Matron part of your title?' She looks confused, so I elaborate. 'Maybe there are different types of nurse, and you are a matron nurse. Or there are different types of matron, and you are a nurse matron.'

'I see what you mean.' She picks up one of my pillows

and punches it. 'I haven't really thought about it. My title is Nurse Matron, so I must be a nurse matron.'

I nod.

'But then again, my surname is actually Matron, so it could be either.'

'Or a bit of both,' Continence says.

Nurse Matron walks round the bed and picks up one of my wife's pillows and punches it.

'Nurse Matron,' I say, and she walks back round the bed and picks up my other pillow and punches it.

'Nurse Matron,' my wife says, trying not to smile.

'Nurse Matron,' I say, laughing out loud.

This time, Nurse Matron stops at the foot of the bed, parks her big hands on her big hips. 'I cannot attend to you both at once.'

Fortunately for her, she doesn't have to, as Professor Smarter has just come in. 'May I have a few minutes with the patients, Nurse Matron?'

Nurse Matron administers another round of hugs, punches our pillows, and leaves the room.

'She's very fat, isn't she.' Professor Smarter says, tugging his thin beige beard. 'Now, I came here to talk to you about brain cancer, otherwise known as cancer of the brain, and my role as head of research at Brain Cancer Research.' He looks at his watch, then up at the door. 'But that will have to wait until another time. Doctor Mann is here, to administer the brain cancer treatment.'

Doctor Mann is the ladylike lady doctor who dresses like a man. She has an assistant with her, of no determinable gender, who carries a white plastic toolbox. The assistant puts the toolbox on the bed, opens the lid and proceeds to remove the tools. For several horrifying seconds, I fear that Doctor

Mann will be using them all, but then the assistant removes the final tool, puts the others back in and closes the lid.

'What are you going to do with that?'

Doctor Mann looks at me. 'Are you going to be my big brave boy?'

I nod.

'Good. Pull down your pyjama bottoms and turn on to your front, on your hands and knees.'

There is something embarrassing about wearing pyjamas while in the company of those dressed in their daywear, particularly if your pyjama top is decorated with characters from a science-fiction television series, but having to remove them, even partially, is far, far worse. My initial instinct is to flee, but wherever I go, the brain cancer is sure to follow. So I get on to my hands and knees, my bottom in the air, and pull down my pyjama bottoms at the back, just far enough to reveal my lower back.

'All the way down. Or do I have to call Nurse Matron?'

I pull them down a bit more.

'Further. I want to see your balls.'

As I reluctantly obey, the assistant prepares the tool, filling it with some sort of white medicated cream.

'This won't hurt a bit.' Doctor Mann puts on a pair of medical gloves, pushes one of her fingers into my anus, slides it in and out several times, then pulls it out, slides in the tool, pulls the trigger, and slides it back out. 'There,' she says, slapping my cheeks, 'all done.'

I pull up my pyjama bottoms.

Nurse Matron turns to my wife, who, not wanting to delay the treatment any further, is already on her hands and knees, stark naked, her bottom exposed to the antiseptic air.

I mutter something about discretion, suggesting that the assistant turn his or her back, but then the door opens and the man with the clipboard comes in. 'Doctor Mann, would you mind if I bring in a group of medical students?'

'Fine with us,' Doctor Mann says.

The medical students shuffle in. There are at least a dozen of them, all male, three of them black. The man with the clipboard is about to close the door when someone else comes in, one of the doctors from the previous day, Doctor Giraffe I think. This time, I get a proper look at him. He does have strange hands, as my wife has said. He's very tall, and wears a white medical coat and sunglasses. A quick word with the man with the clipboard and he joins the group of medical students at the foot of the bed.

'Doctor Mann,' the man with the clipboard says, 'if you would like to—' He stops. The door has opened again, and a young lady comes in. 'Yes, what is it?'

'Sorry to disturb you, but the television crew have arrived.'

The man with the clipboard tucks the clipboard under his arm and slaps himself on the forehead. 'I had completely forgotten. Just send them in.' As the film crew wheel in their camera, boom mike and lights, he explains that they are filming a documentary to be screened peak time on Saturday night, and that we should behave as though they were not present.

'Right.'

The assistant prepares the tool, wiping it on a medicated tissue and filling it with more of the white medicated cream.

Putting on a fresh pair of medical gloves, Doctor Mann pushes one of her fingers into my wife's anus, then a second, then a third. She slides them in and out several times, then pulls them out, slides in the tool, pulls the trigger, and slides it back out.

The medical students nod their heads. One of them raises his hand. He has a question.

'Yes?'

'Is this treatment for bum cancer, or brain cancer?'

'Brain cancer,' Doctor Mann tells him.

'Then why—'

He stops. White medicated cream is squirting out of my wife's ears. I put a hand to the side of my face, then hunt around for some tissues.

Late that night, I wake up, needing the toilet. I am unsure where I am at first, then I recall that I'm in hospital, and that the toilet is just down the corridor, on the right.

I wriggle out from beneath my wife's arm, hang my head over the side of the bed and reach beneath it for my alien-shaped slippers. In the moonlight, they look just like two space aliens, or a pair of space aliens. I slip them on over my feet, stand up, straighten my pyjamas and cross the room to the door.

In the toilet, I stand at the urinal and urinate. Or try to, but someone comes in and I get stage fright. He looks like some sort of superhero. I don't look at him directly, as it is dangerous to look at another man in the toilet, particularly if the man is wearing sky-blue tights.

Out in the corridor, I see him again, leaning against the wall, holding an unlit cigarette. 'Excuse me, have you got a light?'

'Use your super powers,' I say drily. Up close, I can see that he isn't a superhero at all, but a man dressed up as a superhero. He has a beer belly and bandy legs. 'Are you all right? Would you like me to call a nurse?'

He looks me up and down, noting my pyjamas and alien-shaped slippers. 'You're the patient. I'm here on business.'

'Oh, I thought you had escaped from the mental ward.'

'Are you trying to be funny?'

'I am too tired for jokes,' I say, missing the point. 'I simply meant that you look like a mental patient. Nothing more, nothing less.'

He folds his arms across his chest, across the tight T-shirt emblazoned with the letter C, in a superhero declaration of defiance. 'Is this because of my costume?'

I glance down at his sky-blue tights. 'Well, you must admit, you do look a bit odd.'

'You wouldn't say that if I really was a superhero.'

'If you really were a superhero, I wouldn't need to,' I counter, 'as you wouldn't exist.'

He spits on to the linoleum. 'I'm better at peeing than you are.'

'And that makes you a superhero, does it?'

'No, but it does make me more of a man.'

I laugh. Not too loud— he might hit me.

The superhero scowls again, and says: 'I could drink you under the table any day.'

'I doubt that.'

He looks at his watch. 'The bar is still open.'

'What bar?'

'The hospital bar.'

'Oh.'

'I may be recovering from brain cancer,' I say, as he orders two pints of beer, 'but I do know that there is no such thing as a superhero.'

'I'm not saying there is.' He hands me my pint and leads me to an empty table. 'You asked me what I do, and I told you. I help those in need.'

'And what are those in need in need of?'

'Help.'

'Yes, but what sort of help?'

He takes a puff or a drag or whatever it is called from his cigarette. 'Relief.'

'What sort of relief?'

'You do ask a lot of questions. Some of us have just finished work.'

'But what sort of relief?'

'Hand, oral, whatever. I work for a male escort agency. I get paid to satisfy people sexually.'

'Oh, how sleazy.'

'No,' he says defensively. 'It's glamorous. Dining with the rich and famous. Jet-setting all over the world.'

'But this is a hospital.'

'Look around you. What could be more glamorous than this?'

Actually, it is rather glamorous. The floor is of white marble, the tables polished glass, and the concealed lighting is so concealed that you can't even see it. At the bar, world-class brain surgeons sip cocktails, chatting up the patients whose lives they saved just hours before.

'Why jet-set all over the world when everything I could possibly want is right here, in this hospital?'

I nod, catching on. 'You mean the pretty nurses, don't you. You get paid to have sex with the pretty nurses.' I consider this for a moment, then say: 'Why would the pretty nurses pay you for sex?'

'I never said anything about pretty nurses.'

'Well, who then?'

He stubs out his cigarette, gulps down his entire pint, strikes a health-service match and lights another cigarette. 'The patients.'

'That sounds more feasible.'

'The disabled ones mostly. Some of them can't even lift their right arm,' he says sadly. 'The really unlucky ones don't even have a right arm.'

'Oh dear.'

'It's the elderly ones I feel sorry for. Their spouses have died, and they can't exactly go out on the pull.'

'You have sex with old people?'

'Well, who doesn't.'

'I don't,' I say indignantly. 'In fact, most people don't. Even most old people don't.'

'Anyway, it's not about sex, it's about making the world a better place. Imagine, spending your days confined to your bed, eyeing up the pretty nurses, unable to relieve yourself.'

'You're talking about men, aren't you. You have sex with men.' He doesn't answer, so I say: 'All right, tell me about the costume.'

'It excites them. To a disabled person, the ability to walk or to swing from the lampshade is like the ability to leap tall buildings in a single bound. I may look like an idiot to you, but to them I'm a hero.'

'Do you do that? Swing from the lampshade?'

'I do whatever they tell me.'

'And one of them told you to swing from the lampshade.'

He nods. 'It was her thing.'

'Are you sure she wasn't humouring you?'

'Don't ask me,' he says. 'I don't understand women. To be perfectly honest, they make me sick.'

'You sound bitter.'

He spits. 'Well, wouldn't you be? Look at James over there. Just because he's good-looking, they all want to sleep with him. The pretty nurses. And then there's me. Doing it with funny-shaped people, and people who can't wake up.'

'Who is this James person?'

He nods across the bar. 'James Giraffe, the new doctor.'

'Oh, with the sunglasses.' He's sat on a long leather sofa, three pretty nurses on either side, caressing him and reaching up to tickle his chin. 'He seems very popular.'

'The rest of us can't get a look in. Everywhere I go, there's a pretty nurse in tears, saying how he broke her heart, how he dumped her for her best friend, that sort of thing.'

'It sounds like they should steer well clear.'

'You try telling them that. They call him a cad and say how much they hate him, how they never want to see him again. Then they bump into him in the corridor and gaze up into his big brown eyes and go all to pieces. It makes me sick.'

'How can they gaze up into his big brown eyes? He wears sunglasses.'

'He takes them off.'

'Even so, he's so tall, they would need a chair.'

'Not with eyes like that. James has eyes that can melt knickers.'

'Then maybe he's the one with the super powers.' This prompts another scowl, so I say: 'Personally, I don't even think he's that good-looking.'

'James has very unconventional good looks. He has that odd complexion, and a big nose. But it doesn't mean a thing. It's all in the eyes, and the swagger.'

'Swaggering is easy. I can swagger.' I stand up, take a few steps, and fall over. 'That was the beer.'

'You haven't drunk any yet.'

'It's very gassy,' I explain. 'I think I must have inhaled.'

'Let me help you out.' He picks up my pint and downs it in one. 'We should get drunk,' he slurs. 'It's your round.'

I pat the sides of my pyjamas. 'I don't have any cash.'

'Put it on my tab. Captain Cape, sex superhero,' he says, holding out his hand for me to shake. 'Though you can call me Jonathan.'

'Scott Spectrum.'

At the bar, the barmaid doesn't even notice me, as she is busy snogging one of the brain surgeons. After about ten minutes, she stops to catch her breath and comes over. I am about to order the drinks when a nurse appears, tall, blonde and pretty. 'Do you mind if I go first? I'm with James.'

'Go ahead.'

She orders five beers and six cocktails, then looks at me and says: 'The beers are for you-know-who.'

'It must be thirsty work, being popular.'

She sighs. 'Poor James.'

'Why poor James?'

'I shouldn't really say,' she says mysteriously. 'He told us in confidence.'

'Us?'

She indicates her five female friends.

'He told all of you?'

She nods, her face red. 'He confided in us. I think he is learning to open up.'

'I didn't even know he was closed down. I mean, closed in.'

'He's the strong silent type,' she says. 'We want to domesticate him.'

'Good luck.'

'And help him with his problem.'

'What problem?'

She smiles.

'Oh, this is the part he told you in confidence.'

She gazes down at her sensible shoes. 'If I tell you, do you promise not to tell anyone?'

I nod.

'James is impotent,' she whispers. 'The only way he can be cured is if six girls undress in front of him, bend over, and urinate.'

I laugh.

'No wonder James has to drink so much,' she snaps. 'He must get lonely, with everyone being so jealous.' She grabs her tray of drinks and storms off.

When we leave the bar, Cape is so drunk that he can barely stand. I offer to walk him to the hospital exit, but he says that he has to fetch something from his office. 'I didn't even know you had an office.'

'I'm Captain Cape, superhero.'

I nod.

'Look, a pretty nurse. I will use my super powers to chat her up.'

I ask him if this is really a good idea, and suggest that maybe she will mistake him for a drunken fool, but he has already made his approach.

'Good evening.'

The pretty nurse is pushing a metal trolley with a dead boy on it, a price label tied to his big toe. 'What do you mean, good evening? It's three in the morning.'

'Then you must be almost finished your shift.'

'What is it to you?'

'I thought you might like to get together.' He holds out his hand. 'Cape. Captain Cape.'

She keeps both hands on the trolley.

'So how about it? We could go to the park.'

'My mum told me never go to the park with a superhero.'

'I'm not really a superhero.'

'I know. I was humouring you.'

I nudge his arm. 'You need to watch for that.'

He scowls at me, then puts his arm round the pretty nurse, looks down at the dead boy and says: 'That guy looks all partied out.'

She says nothing, shakes her head.

'Let me help you push that.' As he tries to remove her left hand from the trolley handle, he notices her ring. 'Oh, you're married.'

'Engaged.' She holds up the ring. The diamond is the size of an eyeball.

'Dump him,' Cape says assertively. 'You can go out with me instead.'

'If you think I would dump James for you—'

'James?'

'James Giraffe, the enigmatic medical professional. Now if you don't mind—' And she heads off down the corridor, pushing the trolley.

Cape claps his hands. 'Right. Time to smash up my office.'

'I thought you were just going to collect something?'

He shakes his head.

'Then at least let me help. You're in no fit state to smash up anything.' I follow him down the corridor, down another corridor, down another corridor, then, finally, in through a door. 'This is posh,' I say, switching on the light.

'I'm a superhero.'

'I still don't see why you would need an office.'

'Every superhero needs an office. They work there during

the day, in a business suit, then change into their superhero costume when something exciting happens.' He kicks over the rubbish bin, displacing countless crumpled sweet wrappers, then walks round behind the desk and pulls out the desk drawer, upending pens and pencils on to the carpet. 'Are you going to help me or what?'

'I don't really like smashing things up.'

'How can you not like it? There's that famous quote. When a man is tired of smashing things up he is tired of life, for there are loads of things to smash up.'

'Well, if you put it like that—'

'Anyway, it's a good way to let off steam.'

I squint at a row of framed certificates. 'What are these certificates? I'm not wearing my spectacles.'

Cape thinks for a moment, then says: 'Sex school.'

'I thought they might be from superhero college.'

'Same thing.' He picks up the potted rubber plant and pulls out the plant, scattering the room with earth.

'You'll regret this in the morning,' I muse. 'You will wake up tomorrow and think, now why did I do that.'

Cape drops his tights and squats over the waste-paper basket. 'There is no tomorrow.'

'Are you doing a poo?' I open the window, just in case.

'Have you got any loo roll?'

I pass Cape a notebook. 'Use this.'

'Thanks.'

'I'm getting quite into this anarchy lark,' I say, picking my nose and wiping the pickings on to my pyjamas. 'I want to smash something up, but I don't know what to smash up.' I grab a picture from the front of the desk. 'Why do you have a photograph of Doctor Giraffe on your desk? Cape, are you sure this is your office?' I open the office door and squint at the nameplate. Dr Giraffe, PhD, OBE. 'Cape, this is the wrong office.'

He stands up, pulls up his tights.

'You knew, didn't you? I bet you haven't even got an office. It was a trick.'

'I'm drunk. And I wish I was dead.'

'That's no excuse. Look at what you did to this plant.' I lift up the rubber plant and put it back in the rubber plant pot. 'Cape, I want you to put everything back the way you found it.'

'Why should I?'

'Because when Doctor Giraffe sees it, he will call the police.'

'I don't care.'

'Well, I do. I don't want to go to prison.'

'You sort it out then.' I watch him waddle off down the corridor, looking more than ever like a superhero who has lost his super powers, and who has no friends.

The next day, at visiting time, my best friend Vic Twenty comes to visit.

How to describe him. Yes, Vic is like me, only more so. Unsurprisingly, my wife doesn't like him, and has instructed me not to let him into the room. That is why I am sat out here, out in the corridor.

Vic waves at me from the far end of the corridor, then walks towards me and waves again, right up close to my face, a joke he always does. He asks me how I am, and how I have been.

'Fine,' I tell him. 'The brain cancer is in retreat.'

'I knew you would fight it.'

'I didn't fight it exactly. The doctor treated it, with anti-brain-cancer cream.'

'I never knew there was such a thing. How did they administer it?'

'Um, internally,' I say, skirting the issue. Women feel comfortable with intimate subject matter. They don't just talk about each other's orifices, they show each other each other's orifices. They compare orifices, and compare notes. Men are different. Away from the rugby pitch, it is rare for men to see each other naked. And rightly so. The male body is a powerful weapon, and should be handled with care.

Vic reaches for the door handle and says: 'Is this your room?'

'Yes, but you can't go in, or my wife will die.'

'Oh.'

'We could go for a walk around the hospital gardens.'

Vic steps behind me and pulls my chair away from the wall, and I notice that the chair is on wheels, that it is a wheelchair. As I glide along the corridor, it strikes me that I should tell Vic that I can walk, but the chair is so comfortable and the movement so hypnotic that I keep forgetting to tell him. Even now, as we approach the hospital lift, I am forgetting to tell him.

'You're heavy,' Vic says, as he eases the chair over the metal door frame. He considers the array of buttons. 'Which way are the hospital gardens?'

'Ask a member of staff.'

A nurse steps into the lift, so Vic asks her. 'Outside,' she tells him.

'Is that up, or down?'

'Down,' the nurse explains patiently. 'Go to the ground floor, then go outside.'

When I told you that Vic Twenty is like me only more so, I should have said that he is like me only less so. I often forget how socially inept he can be. Vic is a computer programmer, and like all computer programmers, he is good at computer programming and hopeless at everything else.

On reaching the ground floor, Vic eases the chair over the metal door frame and wheels me across the lobby to the entrance, or exit. 'Ramp or stairs?'

'Ramp.' He wheels me down the ramp, a longer route than the stairs but smoother and therefore more suited to those of us who are on wheels.

'I bet you will be glad to get back on your feet again,' Vic says as we reach the bottom of the ramp. 'How long have you been in the wheelchair?'

'About ten minutes.'

'And when did you have the treatment?'

'Yesterday,' I tell him.

'And the brain cancer is already in retreat?'

I nod.

Vic considers this for a moment. 'I had always thought that brain cancer was a serious illness. It's beginning to sound more like a hobby. Do they happen to know what caused it?'

'It is impossible to know for sure, but it may have been caused by our next-door neighbour's television aerial, the tallest television aerial in the world.'

'Is this anything to do with the ghost giraffe?'

'Oh, you mean Jim. I'd forgotten all about Jim.'

'How did you two meet? You never said.'

'He just turned up one night, in the wardrobe,' I say, thinking back. 'We got talking, and that was it.'

'You became good friends.'

'I wouldn't go that far. He was very critical, for a giraffe. He kept saying that I work too hard, and that I am sexually repressed. He said that if I don't change my ways, I will die of a heart attack.'

'You're too young to die of a heart attack, Scott.'

'He got one thing right though,' I concede. 'He told me that the television aerial would give me brain cancer, and it did.'

'Even so, I wouldn't take health advice from a ghost.'

I nod, smile. It is hard to think about death out here, in the lush green surrounds of the hospital gardens. Here we are lost among the boxy hedges of the star-shaped hospital maze. And here we are at the fountain, with its stone fish spitting fish-pleasing water. And here we are walking down a stony pathway through sun-dappled woodland, where I catch a snatch of dialogue from behind the bushes.

'Oh, James, you're an animal.'

'Grr.'

Vic and I each turn a blind eye or two. The wheelchair stops only momentarily, presumably so that Vic can shake his head in disgust, and we press on, along the stony pathway, up out of the woodland and on to the side of a hill. Neither of us has spoken for some time, when Vic says: 'So when was the last time you saw him?'

'Who?'

'Jim, the ghost giraffe.'

I scratch my head in thought. 'It was round about the time that I developed brain cancer.'

'Then Jim is what you would call a fairweather friend.'

'I think friend might be pushing it, Vic. Mind you, I doubt I have seen the last of him. If anyone can be likened to a bad smell, it is Jim Giraffe.'

*   *   *

'Has he gone?' Continence asks me, as Nurse Matron punches our pillows.

'You don't like my best friend, do you.'

Continence shakes her head, then stops shaking it, lifts up her straight brown hair and asks me to pass her her round brown hair-tie. I pass it to her and she ties it round her brown hair, tying it in a straight brown shape. 'Nurse Matron says we can go home soon.'

'How soon?'

'We have to go in and see one of the senior doctors for a consultation, some time this afternoon.' She looks at her watch, at the round brown clock face. 'Now, in fact.'

'That is correct. Mrs Spectrum, you will be seeing a lady doctor, Doctor Mann. Mr Spectrum, you come with me.'

I follow Nurse Matron down the corridor, down another corridor, down another corridor, down another corridor, then, finally, down another corridor. She knocks on a door, a great oak door built of solid oak, opens the door, pushes me inside, and closes the door.

The room is constructed almost entirely of oak. Much of the floor space is taken up by a great oak desk, sat at which is a rather nondescript-looking woman. At her side, in his usual white medical coat and sunglasses, is Doctor Giraffe. The woman invites me to take a seat, but there is no seat, so I remain standing. I stand here for more than a minute, folding and unfolding my arms, until finally the enigmatic medical professional whispers something into the woman's nondescript ear. His ear is an odd shape, pointy, with tufts of orange hair. His other ear is the same, though in reverse.

'Doctor Giraffe will not be speaking to you directly,' the woman tells me. 'Doctor Giraffe does not speak to male patients. If you wish to speak to Doctor Giraffe, speak to me and I will speak to Doctor Giraffe on your behalf. Is that understood?'

I nod.

'Answer yes, or no.'

'Yes.' Again, nothing is said for more than a minute, so I say: 'I would like to ask Doctor Giraffe when I will be allowed home.'

Doctor Giraffe wrinkles his nose in thought, then turns his head and whispers something to the woman, who tells me: 'Doctor Giraffe says that you can go home when you are better, and not before.'

'Could you ask Doctor Giraffe when that might be?'

'Doctor Giraffe says that it depends on the results of the urine test.'

'Then will you please ask Doctor Giraffe when we can expect to receive the results of the test.'

Doctor Giraffe looks down at a sheet of paper on the desk.

'Doctor Giraffe has the test results in front of him now,' the woman says.

'Well, what are the results?' I demand, loosening my pyjama collar.

Doctor Giraffe reads a sentence from the sheet of paper, following the words with one of his odd hands, then whispers something into the woman's ear, good news I hope.

'The news is good,' the woman tells me. 'Your brain cancer has been cured. You can go home.'

I smile, and breathe a sigh of relief. 'Phew.'

But Doctor Giraffe is whispering again.

'The news is not all good,' the woman tells me. 'Your brain cancer has been cured, but you are still going to die. The test results show that you are sexually repressed, that the sexual repression is putting a strain on your heart, and that you will die of a heart attack.'

'Oh,' I say, not pleased. 'Can anything be done? An operation, perhaps, or therapy—'

Doctor Giraffe stands up and crosses the room to a great oak bookcase. He pulls down a huge oak-bound book, carries it back to his chair, flicks through, reads silently to himself, then, once again, whispers into the nondescript ear of the nondescript woman.

'There is a highly specialised technique known as jimming,' the woman explains. 'It involves developing the sexual appetite while simultaneously broadening the range of sexual experiences. You, Mr Spectrum, must perform every sex act in the lovemaker's lexicon. Only then will the pressure be lifted from your heart and the threat of death be eradicated. And Mr Spectrum—'

'Yes?'

'Close the door on your way out.'

Where did all the fun go?

Continence has gone away for a few days, to stay with her mother. This was my idea, but I cleverly made her think that it was her idea. I told her that I had dreamt that a burglar had broken into her mother's house and laughed at her mother. When Continence asked me if my dreams ever come true, I told her that they do, and she packed her bag.

The moment she is out of the house, I empty out the wardrobe, dumping the contents in the spare room. Then, I put on my trainers, run down to the newsagent's and return with an armful of pornographic magazines. Despite the fact that he talks about sex almost constantly, I do not actually know what Jim is into, so I include all genres. Teens, grannies, boobs, bums, legs, fat, black, hairy, shaven, held open, even readers' wives. I pile them up on the bedroom carpet and run down to the supermarket, where I fill a trolley with cans of beer and half a dozen packets of dry-roasted peanuts. I load it into the back of a taxi, drag it all upstairs and dump it by the wardrobe door. At midnight, I grab my mobile phone and dial the number of the local twenty-four-hour pizza parlour and order a large pizza. Twenty minutes later, I pay the delivery boy, place the pizza box in the bottom of the wardrobe and get into bed.

I must have fallen asleep. The lighting has changed, the sun is starting to show through the window. Sitting up, I can see several crumpled beer cans and a torn peanut packet, the insides licked clean. The pornographic magazines lay scattered across the carpet, many open at the centre pages, some glistening with something sticky and silvery. The wardrobe door is shut, so I rise from my bed to open it, but find only the greasy pizza box and several nibbled crusts.

Needing the toilet, I step into my alien-shaped slippers and cross the landing to the bathroom. I can hear Continence in there, brushing her teeth. Just as I am about to return to my bed, I realise that Continence is staying with her mother, so it can't be her, and if it can't be her then it must be someone else. I knock politely and put my ear to the door.

'Hold on,' says a familiar voice. 'I'm on the loo.'

'But I can hear you brushing your teeth.'

'And your point is—'

I shake my head in disgust. When the door finally opens, I'm here waiting, hands on hips. 'Which toothbrush did you use?'

'The spaceship-shaped one.'

'Jim, that's mine. I'm going to have to throw it away now.'

'There was either that or the soppy pink one.'

I grab my toothbrush from the window sill and give it a

sniff. Leaves. Fresh ones, from the very tops of the trees. 'Ugh.'

'What's up with you?'

'Just knowing that it has been in your mouth, near your dirty mind. And look at the state of the bristles.' I show Jim the bristles. 'Maybe Continence can boil it.'

When I glance up from the toothbrush, Jim is giving me a funny look. I'm not sure at first, but I think it might be a smile. Not a manic grin as you might expect, but a smile. He shakes his head, laughs. 'You haven't changed a bit.'

'How so?'

'You were an anal git last time I saw you, and you're an anal git now.'

'And you're still an oaf.'

'Geek.'

'Mammal.'

'Underpants,' Jim says laterally. 'You got dressed in the dark, and put them on back to front.'

'I wear boxer shorts and you know it. Which reminds me. Do you remember the early days, when you first arrived? You wore a pair of underpants on your head. Just the first few times. Where did you get them?'

'A souvenir from a previous haunting. When I move on from here, it'll be a pair of your boxer shorts.'

'What if you haunt a woman? Do you wear her knickers?'

'I don't want to spoil your fantasies, Spec, but there is no such thing as a transvestite ghost giraffe.'

'I'm glad to hear it.'

He shuffles his hoofs. 'If you do ever catch me dressed in women's clothing, it doesn't mean anything. I'd be wearing them because I don't wear them, as a sort of joke.'

'Irony.'

'No,' he says, shaking his head vigorously, 'I wouldn't iron them. No one irons their undies, Spec.'

'I said irony, as in ironic.'

'Oh, I thought you said iron them. There's no point ironing them, if you're just going to put them on your head—'

'Jim, I didn't say anything about ironing.'

'— and bounce on somebody's bed.'

'I hope you don't bounce on my bed.'

'Only when you're not looking.'

'And that makes it all right, does it? Well, I hope you wipe your hoofs first.'

'Of course,' Jim says. 'I wipe them on your pillow.'

'And you wonder why you're unpopular.'

'Ghosts aren't meant to be popular. Scary, yes. Popular, no.'

'But you're not scary either. You're just annoying.' His response to this is to back up then run at me very fast, pulling a face. I, of course, do not even flinch. 'And what was that supposed to be?'

'Nothing.'

'You were trying to frighten me, weren't you.'

'No.'

'Then why the ludicrous facial contortions?'

He shrugs. 'It was one of them irony things.'

'You haven't got an ironic bone in your body. Not that you have any bones. But if you did have bones, none of them would be ironic.'

'That's what's so ironic about them,' Jim says, clutching at straws. 'They're so ironic, I haven't even got any.'

'Don't try to be clever, Jim, it doesn't suit you.'

'Fair enough.' He turns round and trots into the bedroom.

'Where are you going?'

He shrugs.

'Charming. You come round here, eat my pizza—'

'What do you expect, if you leave it in the wardrobe.'

'Well, I don't expect you to eat it.'

'I'm a creature of instinct. I see a pizza, I eat it.'

'A creature of instinct indeed,' I say, straightening my sceptical spectacles. 'You, Jim, are calculating. As in cold and.'

'And—'

'What?'

'And what?'

'What do you mean, and what?'

'You said I'm cold and,' Jim says. 'Cold and what.'

'Calculating.'

'Eh?'

'Cold and calculating. Jim, you're doing it now. You confuse me, so that I forget what I was trying to say. If you really were a creature of instinct, you wouldn't be so clever, and you wouldn't say such stupid things.'

He licks his nostril.

'You, Jim, possess what is known as selective idiocy. We all know perfectly well how clever you can be,' I say, sitting on the edge of the bed, 'and yet you hide behind this— this laddish façade.'

'You don't like me much, do you?'

I want to say no, I don't. You make my blood boil. But I can't. I need his help. I need him to teach me about sex. 'Of course I like you,' I say, crossing my fingers behind my back.

'What have you got there?'

'Where?'

Jim eyes me with deep suspicion. 'Behind your back.'

'Nothing.'

'Show me.'

I uncross my fingers and hold out an empty hand.

'Were you crossing your fingers?'

'No.'

'Do it again. Tell me you like me, but this time, say it with your hands in your lap, where I can see.'

I rest my hands on the front of my boxer shorts, taking care not to touch anything that might respond. 'Jim, I like you. You're my best friend.'

He doesn't say anything for a moment. Blinks. Trots round the bed, peers behind me, finds nothing there, then trots back. 'Do you mean that?'

I nod, uncrossing my crossed toes.

'But I thought Vic Twenty was your best friend.'

'He was, but when I met you, I relegated him to second place. How do you know about Vic Twenty anyway?'

'By spying on you,' Jim says in a matter-of-fact sort of voice. 'I watched you playing computer games in his house.'

I nod, glazing over. 'Happy days.'

He grimaces. If you have ever seen a giraffe grimace, you will know that it is not a pretty sight. 'Computer games are crap. You're just sat in front of a screen, waggling a stick.'

'Not just any old stick. A joystick, a game controller.'

'It's a stick, a crappy plastic stick. With a red button on top. You move it, and a little man runs across the screen, shooting stupid monsters.'

'They're hardly stupid,' I say in the monsters' defence. 'Have you never heard of artificial intelligence?'

He shakes his head.

'It's like your artificial stupidity, but in reverse.'

He nods.

'In the olden days, the monster followed a set pattern. Your modern monster might hide behind some bushes, wait for you to walk past, then jump out and eat you. Or it might wear a disguise. You're about to leap over a bush when the bush reaches out and grabs you, and you lose a life.'

He raises an eyebrow.

'There might be two monsters stuck together, and you just manage to kill one when the other comes unstuck and kills you. Or it might go invisible, then materialise right in your path, and you walk into it and die.'

Jim doesn't say anything. For once, he actually looks impressed. 'What game is that then?'

'It could be any game. I was just giving an example.'

'Can I play it?'

'Play what?'

'The monster game.'

'It isn't an actual game,' I say, holding my tongue. 'There are lots of games. If you like, I will take you round to Vic's house and you can have a go.'

'Are you serious?'

I shrug.

'The one with the monsters, where they go invisible and jump on you and stuff.'

'It isn't an actual game—'

'But there is one with monsters in it?'

I have to think about this. Vic has so many games, he's what you call a professional gamer, he writes games in his spare time and he works for a computer games company, testing computer games. It is up to Vic to ensure that the game isn't too easy, or too hard. If the game is too easy, they add more monsters or make their teeth bigger, or give them feelers so that they can find you in the dark. If the game is too hard, they get rid of some of the monsters. 'Hmm. There is one called Monsters Are All Over The Place. You control this man—'

Jim pulls a face.

'Don't you want to be a man?'

He shakes his head.

'You want to be a giraffe, don't you.'

He nods.

'Jim, I don't think there are any giraffe games.'

This, of course, does not go down well. He grabs a full can of beer with his teeth and hurls it against the wall.

'Jim—'

He grabs another can and tosses it out through the bedroom door, out on to the landing. I hear it bounce down the stairs, thump thump thump.

'Jim, please.'

But he's facing the wall, in a huff.

'Jim, don't be difficult. If you get a reputation for being difficult, people won't want to work with you any more, and you won't be in the rest of the novel. Would you like a can of beer?' I open a can of beer and waft it under his nose. 'Well, I'll have it then.' I put the beer to my lips and make a slurping sound. 'Mmm,' I say convincingly. 'Yum yum.'

No response.

'Look, Jim, I'm drunk.' I walk in circles, swaying, bumping into things. 'Come on, Jim, have a beer. You're missing the party.' I peer round his nose, at his face. 'Jim, is that a smile? There, in the corner. Under that tuft of unsightly nostril hair.'

He shakes his head. But there was a smile, I saw it.

'Let's order a pizza. Would you like another pizza, Jim?'

'Might do.'

'Do you want extra cheese?' I pick up my mobile phone. Just as I start to dial, an idea strikes. 'Jim, that could be what caused your foul mood. Cheese.'

He turns his head, looks at me, puzzled.

'My mum suffers from it. Give her a cheese sandwich and she'll thank you for it at the time, but an hour later she might just bite your head off.' I pick up my mobile phone again. 'Maybe they do a pizza without any cheese on it. You could have extra toppings.'

'Yuk.'

'What do you mean, yuk?'

'No cheese,' Jim says in a stupid voice.

'It could have oil on it, like garlic bread.'

'I can't eat garlic.'

I shake my head, shaking off the Jim. 'I simply meant that it could be the same sort of bread. Anyway, why can't you eat garlic?'

'I'm allergic.'

'Seriously?'

He nods. 'I'm a ghost. All ghosts are allergic to garlic.'

I pick up one of the pornographic magazines and flick through. 'Hang on,' I say, looking up from the page, 'are you sure you got that right?'

'What?'

'The bit about ghosts being allergic to garlic. I always thought it was vampires. Though with vampires it isn't exactly an allergy. It kills them. Odd really, what with it being an anticoagulant.'

'That's in the films.'

'But where do the films get it from? There must be something in it.'

'It's nothing to do with vampires. It's a giraffe thing, Spec. All giraffes are allergic to garlic.'

'Hang on,' I say, tossing the magazine to the floor, 'you just told me that you're allergic to garlic because you're a ghost. And now you say you're allergic to garlic because you're a giraffe. Make up your mind.'

'It is made up.'

'Ah, so you admit it.'

'No, I mean my mind is made up.'

I fold my arms. 'I'm listening.'

He wrinkles his snout, as though chewing on an unsavoury smell. 'You see, it's like this. I was always allergic to garlic, ever since I was a cub. But I only found out about it last year, when I signed up for the army.'

'I never knew you were in the army.'

'I wasn't. I passed all the fitness tests, even the one where they tie sandbags to your hoofs and chuck you off a cliff. But then came the medical. They rubbed garlic on my flank, and it flared up. So that was it. They wouldn't let me in.'

'Well, how could they? After all, who ever heard of a soldier who can't eat garlic.'

'I can't think of any.'

I nod. It is nice when Jim and I agree on things, even if it is a load of old nonsense. The important thing is that he is here, and that we remain friends. You know what they say. One day, that perverted companion might just save your life. 'Right, let's order that pizza.'

'I don't want one now.'

'Well, what do you want?'

He grins. 'Garlic.'

'But Jim, you're allergic to garlic.'

'I'm dead. What have I got to lose?'

'All right, I've got a tin of garlic soup in the kitchen,' I say, leading him down the stairs. 'There is one problem though. Continence has had a sort-out, so I don't know where anything is. She may even have thrown it away. She hates my garlic soup, says it's the only thing that makes her glad we sleep in separate beds.' I step into the kitchen. 'Jim, what do you think about the separate beds issue?' I enquire, in an attempt at bringing up the subject of sex. The ghost giraffe looks indifferent, so I add: 'Do you think Continence and I ought to sleep together?'

'It's none of my business.'

That's not like him. He must be hungry. The only thing that interests Jim Giraffe more than sex is food. Oh, and beer. 'Jim,' I say, opening the cupboard door, 'you're taller than me, can you see on to the top shelf?'

He sticks his head into the cupboard, his entire head, dislodging some of the tins, which roll out and crash on to the worktop.

'Can you see a tin with the words garlic soup on it, and a picture of a piping-hot bowl of garlic soup?'

'No.'

I sometimes wonder if there is anything in that ethereal head of his. 'Look to the left,' I say. 'Can you see it now?'

'No.'

'To the right?'

'No,' he says. 'No garlic soup.'

Hmm. 'Up periscope. The tins might be piled up, it might be on top of another tin.'

He extends his neck. 'Oh, I've found it.'

'Bring it down then.'

He retrieves his head, bends his neck and places the tin on the worktop.

'Thank you, Jim.' I open a drawer and take out a tin-opener. 'Do you have tinned food in the jungle, Jim? Of course you don't. Because that would be ridiculous, wouldn't it. Mmm, have a sniff of that.' I drop the serrated lid into the rubbish bin and hold the tin to Jim's nose. His eyes turn green. 'Well, that certainly struck a chord. Shall I pop it in the microwave, or heat it on the hob like they used to, in the olden days?'

'Microwave.'

'You can't wait to try it, can you.'

'It's not that. I just like to watch.'

I pour the soup into a bowl, place the bowl in the microwave and press the start button. 'It must be nice to be so easily amused, Jim.'

He doesn't say anything. He's watching it go round.

'I have to take it out now, give it a stir.' I do so, then put it back in.

'Can you make it go faster?'

'I could, but I would have to get in there and push.'

'You wouldn't fit.'

'It was a joke. No need to laugh though, Jim. I wouldn't want you to strain yourself.'

He isn't even listening. He's so engrossed in watching the soup, you could shorten his neck, paint him black and white and change his name to Jim Zebra, and he wouldn't even notice. We hear a ping, and it stops.

'Can you do it again?'

'We mustn't overcook it,' I explain. 'It's a delicate balance of flavours.'

'How can it be a delicate balance of flavours? It's garlic.'

'Not just garlic.'

'What else is in there?'

'Well, there are different types of garlic.'

'Spec, garlic is garlic.'

'Yes,' I say, 'by definition. But there are different methods of preparation. Steamed, grilled, fried, you name it. And there are different shapes of garlic, and different sizes. Also, you can chop it up differently. Some of it isn't chopped up at all. Look at that,' I say, pointing with my finger, 'a whole clove.'

He turns his nose up.

'Don't turn your nose up, Jim. It's ever so rude. If you don't like my cooking—'

'What do you mean, your cooking? It came out of a tin.'

'Yes, but who opened the tin? And set the timer on the microwave?'

'The easy stuff. You didn't make the actual soup.'

'I could have. You've only got to peel some garlic and chuck it in a food processor.'

'What about the delicate mix of flavours, the different methods of preparation, all that caper?'

'Sod that,' I say, stepping out of character. 'Now which do you prefer, a fork or a spoon?'

'Fork.'

'Are you sure? It might seep through, between the prongs.'

'Spoon then.'

'Can you hold a spoon?'

'I can hold anything if I'm hungry enough.'

I put the soup bowl on the worktop, open the cutlery drawer and grab a fork. When I turn round, the bowl is empty, and Jim's snout is tinged white. 'Did you just eat all the garlic soup?'

'What garlic soup?'

'Exactly.'

'It must have evaporated.'

'Jim, garlic soup does not evaporate.'

'It does, Spec. I saw it.'

'Impossible,' I exclaim. 'The air would be thick with it.'

Jim sniffs, and my hair moves.

'Can you smell anything?'

He shakes his head.

'No, because it didn't evaporate at all. You ate it. And you're too stubborn to admit it. Though I can't see why,' I say, knowing something he doesn't. 'It was your soup.'

'Was it?'

'Well, it might as well have been. Continence says I'm not allowed to eat garlic soup.'

'Where is Continence anyway?'

'At her mother's. Just for a few days.'

'Have you two had a row?'

'We never row,' I say proudly. 'We wouldn't know how to.'

'It's good for you,' Jim says. 'Calling each other a cunt. Throwing stuff. Any of that caper.'

'Do you know, a marriage-guidance counsellor once told us the same thing. Though she phrased it differently. Come on, she said, get it all out in the open. I told her that she was wrong, and that my wife agreed.'

'So where is she now?'

'Who, the marriage-guidance counsellor?'

'Your wife.'

'At her mother's, like I said.'

Jim nods. Not an ordinary nod, but a clever, knowing nod, a nod which suggests that my marriage is in tatters, that my wife is out of the house purely because I am in it.

'Why are you looking at me like that?'

'I knew it wouldn't last, Spec. You're too different. She says tomato, you don't say anything.'

'And what is that supposed to mean?'

'She's left you. Admit it. She's taken her dildo and buggered off.'

'But Jim—' I begin, but then stop. I can't tell him the truth, that she is away because of the dream I didn't have, as then I would have to mention the plan. I shall make something up. 'Let me explain,' I say, making something up. 'You may have noticed that my bedroom is full of pornographic magazines. They belong to a friend of mine, who asked me to look after them for a bit, while he reorganises his shelves.'

'I wondered where they came from. Is that why she left you, because of the porn?'

'She hasn't left me, Jim.'

'So what about the booze?'

'The cans of beer.' I scratch my nose, stalling for time. 'I won those cans of beer in a raffle.'

'And the pizza?'

'Um. The delivery boy brought it by mistake. So I put it in the wardrobe.' Jim looks unconvinced, so I add: 'They have this new delivery boy, and he isn't very good.'

'So she left you for the pizza-delivery boy. Well, you can't blame her, Spec. All that free pizza.'

'For the last time, Continence has not left me. With all these weird goings on going on, I just thought she was best off out of the house.'

'What weird goings on?'

'The magazines, the pizza, the ghost giraffe. Oh, and the beer.'

'Nothing weird about beer, Spec. Mind you, things do get

a bit weird, if you drink too much. You start seeing things. There you are, lying in bed, feeling a bit nauseous, when suddenly, as if by magic, your shoes turn into a toilet.'

'You don't wear shoes.'

'And now you know why. Anyway, you still haven't told me why you two broke up.'

'Jim, our marriage is as strong as the day we signed the forms.'

'Then why is she at her mother's?'

I sigh a deep, weary sigh. 'The truth is, Jim,' I begin, 'Continence is, um, sunbathing. At her mother's house. Yes, her mother has a new sunbed. She won it. In a raffle.'

'Is this the same raffle where you won the pizza?'

'The beer,' I correct. 'The pizza was delivered by mistake. Actually, it was the pizza boy who sold us the tickets. He thought, while I'm delivering pizza I might as well sell a few raffle tickets. To raise money. For the pizza-relief fund. Jim, why are you laughing?'

He's rolling about on the kitchen floor, kicking the ceiling with his hoofs, laughing his metaphorical socks off. 'Pizza-relief fund. Raffle tickets. I've never heard so much bollocks in all my life.'

'Jim, calm down. Jim—' He's coughing, spluttering, clutching his tall yellow throat with his hoofs. 'Jim, what is it?'

He tries to speak, but can't.

'Let me get you a pillow.'

I run upstairs, grab a pillow from the bedroom, run back down and place it under his head. The head moves, so I move the pillow, but it moves again, so I move the pillow again and it moves again. The entire ghost giraffe has gone into spasm.

'Jim, it wasn't that funny. It wasn't even a joke. Not that

you laugh at jokes. Well, you never laugh at my jokes. Jim, shall I call the doctor? I shall call the doctor.' I run into the lounge, grab the telephone and call Doctor Apple. 'Sorry to wake you, Doctor Apple, but a friend of mine is having a rather irritating fit. He was laughing at one of my jokes,' I explain, 'and he got a bit carried away. Colour, what do you mean what colour?'

Back in the kitchen, Jim is stood at the sink, his head under the cold tap. His face is purple. His whole body is purple, with pink spots. 'Garlic.'

'There's none left,' I tell him. 'I shall go to the shop.'

'No,' he splutters. 'Garlic. Allergy.'

'Oh.' I run back to the lounge. 'Doctor Apple,' I say into the receiver, 'it seems that my friend has eaten some garlic, and that he has a garlic allergy. Yes, Doctor Apple. No, Doctor Apple.' I thank him for his time, and hang up.

'What did he say?' Jim is stretched out on the kitchen floor, his head between his legs, performing some kind of resuscitation manoeuvre. Or maybe he is just trying to take his mind off it.

'You are to get plenty of rest, and taken an aspirin.'

'Fuck that,' Jim says defiantly. 'I'm off to the pub.'

'You shouldn't drink alcohol during a period of illness, Jim.'

'Best thing for it. Flushes out all the poisons.'

'But alcohol is a poison.'

'Yes, so it stimulates the immune system.'

'But Jim, alcohol is an immunosuppressant.'

'Beer is sterile,' Jim says, clutching at straws. 'It kills all the germs.'

'What germs? You're just lying to yourself, so that you can drink beer without feeling guilty.'

'Bollocks.'

'Excuse me?'

'Bollocks.'

'Now look me in the eye and say that.'

'Boll—'

He can't.

'Balls.'

'Well that's hardly the same thing.' I fold my arms. 'All right. It's your body, Jim. If you want to spend the rest of your weekend in hospital—'

'Don't say that.'

'Do you not like hospitals, Jim?'

'I don't know,' he says. 'I've never been in one.'

'I have, and believe me, it isn't nice.'

He frowns.

'Jim, do you remember the warning you gave me about next door's television aerial? You told me that it would give me brain cancer. I mocked you at the time, but you were right. I did develop brain cancer. My wife did, too. We went into hospital, where we were successfully treated with anti-cancer cream.'

Jim eyes me curiously. 'How does that work?'

'Anti-cancer cream? It infiltrates the brain and destroys the cancer.'

'But how do they get it into your brain, Spec? Do they inject it directly into your brain?'

I lean against the fridge, for support. 'Um. They don't take a direct route, no.'

He grins. 'They squirted it up your arse, didn't they.'

'You're obsessed. Here I am telling you how I almost died, and all you are interested in is unusual anal insertions. I'm beginning to wonder if you're not a closet homosexual.'

'A wardrobe homosexual.'

'Whatever.'

'How about your wife? Did they squirt it up her arse, too?'

'We both underwent similar treatment, yes.'

'Was it a lady doctor, or a man doctor?'

'A lady doctor. And no, Jim, that does not make my wife a lesbian. I can't win, can I? If it had been a man doctor, you would make some joke about him pumping her full of cream.'

'So she saw your wife's cunt?'

'Lots of people saw it,' I say, playing it down. 'It was broadcast on national television.'

'You're pulling my neck.'

'There were some medical students, if I recall.'

'Anyone else?'

'No. Well, there was one other doctor, Doctor Giraffe.'

'Giraffe.'

'Yes. Oh,' I exclaim, making the connection, 'he was your namesake.'

'His first name wasn't Jim, was it?'

'Now that would be spooky. His name was James, and he was a highly respected medical professional.'

'Not like me then.'

'He looked a bit like you actually.'

Jim laughs. 'Maybe it was me in disguise.'

I laugh, too.

'Was he tall?'

'Um,' I say, thinking back, 'actually, he was rather tall. He was terribly good-looking. Though that may have been the sunglasses. And he was sweet and charming, so not really like you at all.'

Jim frowns.

'And he would never have done anything stupid like eat something to which he is allergic. And turn purple with pink spots. He was far too cool for that.'

'Did you fancy him?'

'Of course not,' I state firmly. 'Mind you, everyone else did. He was a big hit with the ladies, if I remember.'

Jim nods, taking this all in. I wonder if he might be envious, if maybe Jim is not the ladies' man— or ladies' giraffe— he would have us believe. He may even be shy. Yes, that's it, he's shy. No wonder he acts the fool. I was like that myself once, before I married. Marriage brings confidence with women, confidence which would have come in handy when one was single. This is one of life's cruellest ironies. 'Jim,' I say suddenly, 'do you enjoy being single?'

'Why do you ask?'

'It is a long time since I was last on the scene, and I was wondering what it's like out there.'

Jim hangs his head. 'Get dressed,' he says quietly. 'We're going to the pub.'

Toilet Tart

Being the stay-at-home type, I am not familiar with the local pub scene, so I take Jim to a bright accessible chain pub called the Slag & Cabbage. 'This place is packed out on a Friday night,' I say, pressing my spectacles against the glass. 'It looks a bit empty at the moment though.'

'It's five o'clock on a Sunday morning,' Jim says.

'Then why did you suggest we go for a drink?'

'Follow me.'

'Where to exactly?'

'One of my favourite, um, haunts,' he jokes. He turns on his hoofs and trots off up the road.

'Jim,' I pant, catching him up, 'please don't tell me we are about to enter the Bad Leg.'

'It's the only place open. They do what we call a lock-in,' he explains. 'When it gets to chucking-out time, instead of chucking you out, they lock you in.'

'That's not very nice.'

'It is if you're an alcoholic.'

'Even alcoholics need to sleep at night, Jim.'

'They lock the doors to stop people coming in, not going out.'

'And what if somebody informs the police?'

'The police already know about it, Spec.'

'Then why don't they have it closed down?'

'They can't. Where else would they get a late-night drink?'

I put my hands into my trouser pockets, in a ho-hum sort of way, and say: 'All right, smart neck, but there is one thing you haven't thought of. If there is a lock-in—'

'Yes?'

'— then the doors will be locked. And if the doors are locked—'

'Yes?'

'— and we're outside—'

'Yes?'

'— then we can't get in.'

'Oh.'

'And another thing.' I tap the glass, drawing his atten-tion to a small cardboard sign. It states that dogs are not allowed on the premises, and is illustrated with a cartoon of a rather dejected-looking dog.

'I have drunk here before, you know. I do know what I'm doing.'

'Then how do you usually get in?'

'I'm a ghost, I can go where I like.'

'Great,' I say, flicking my fringe with heavy sarcasm. 'And what am I supposed to do?'

'I'll let you in through the toilet window, at the back.'

I peer round the corner of the building, into the car park. 'There might be prostitutes.'

'You keep your money in your pocket.'

'I simply meant that I might get propositioned.'

'Just swat them away, like this,' Jim says, swishing his tail.

'You're thinking of flies. Prostitutes are human beings. More or less. And ought to be treated with respect.'

'Have you ever been with a prostitute then, Spec?'

'I would rather die.'

'We'll soon see about that,' Jim says mysteriously, before passing even more mysteriously through the closed pub door.

At the rear of the building, I cross the dimly lit car park to the pub's back wall, where I find two small frosted-glass windows, one of which must be the window to the Gents. Just as I am about to scratch my head and wonder which it might be, one of the windows opens and Jim's nostrils appear, gaping rudely. 'In you come.'

'How am I supposed to get up there?'

'Climb on something.'

'There isn't anything to climb on.'

'Nothing? Nothing at all?'

'No. Well,' I concede, 'only the rubbish bins. Nothing clean.'

'Stand on one of the bins.'

'But Jim, they haven't even got lids.'

'Well, what else is there?'

I step back. Looking up, I can see the sky, dark blue, dotted with rain. Behind me, there's the row of parked cars, and a prostitute. There isn't anything else, just the two rubbish bins, one half empty, one half full. 'Jim,' I say in the familiar loud whisper, 'I have an idea. If I empty one of the rubbish bins into the other rubbish bin, I can stand on top of the rubbish and climb in through the window.'

'Don't talk about it, Spec. Do it.'

I take off my Space Man In Space Series Two sweat-shirt, fold it, and place it carefully on the window ledge. Next, I pick up one of the rubbish bins, the one that is half empty, and tip the rubbish into the one that is half full. The bin is heavy and hurts my back, but it is worth the sacrifice as I want to be with Jim. I put on my sweat-shirt and climb up into the bin, balancing precariously on the topmost items of rubbish, namely, an industrial-sized baked-bean tin and an inverted margarine tub, then pull myself up and in through the window. In the stark blue glare of the naked light bulb— and the naked ghost giraffe— I can see what a mess I have got myself in. 'Damn,' I say, slipping into the vernacular. 'And these were clean trousers, too.'

'I wouldn't have done it like that.'

'How would you have done it, clever neck?'

'Emptied one out, turned it upside down and stood on the bottom.'

'Jim, why didn't you tell me that before?'

He shrugs.

'Oh, like that, is it? I thought we were friends. I mean, look. We've gone to the pub together. That makes us drinking partners.'

'And we're hanging out in the toilets,' Jim says. 'Which makes us bum chums.'

'Are you so insecure in your sexuality that you can't even chat to another man in the men's lavatory without feeling threatened?'

'Well, if you keep going on about sex—'

'I never said anything about sex. I was talking in very general terms about sexuality.'

'What are you doing?'

'Unzipping my fly and exposing my penis.'

'Spec, we should swap places.'

'How do you mean?'

'I'm supposed to be the ghost, and you're scaring me.'

'If you think I'm doing this for your benefit,' I say, urinating into the urinal, 'you're mistaken.' I direct the flow of urine on to a soggy cigarette butt, propelling it into the plughole. When I look up, Jim is staring at me. 'Would you like me to perform a song-and-dance routine?'

'Eh?'

'Well, seeing as I have an audience. Jim, why don't you go to the counter—'

'The bar.'

'Whatever. And order some drinks.'

'I thought I should keep an eye on you.'

'I can go to the toilet on my own you know, Jim. Have been doing so since I was eleven.'

'That's not what I'm worried about. Pubs are dangerous places, Spec.'

'How do you mean?'

'Um, I'm not gay or anything—'

'Go on.'

He shuffles his hoofs, something he always does when nervous. 'You're quite pretty for a man. You've got fair hair, and you walk like a girl. Spec, now what are you doing?'

'Overcompensating,' I say, stomping across the tiles. 'I fear for my safety. And I want to go home.'

'You can't go home.'

'Why not?'

'It's a lock-in. We're locked in.'

'But you said—'

'Don't listen to me, Spec. I talk out of my snout.' Jim opens the toilet door, turning the handle with the tip of his tail, and trots out into the pub proper. 'Two pints of beer,' he says to the proletarian barman.

'Jim,' I snap, 'remember your manners.'

'What manners?'

'Do you not have any manners?'

'No.'

'Oh.'

'I'm in a pub, Spec. And when I'm in a pub,' he elaborates, 'the only thing I care about is beer. And women. And having a fight.'

'If you start a fight, Jim, I'm calling the police.'

'You won't have to shout very loud, Spec. They're sat over there, by the jukebox.'

I follow his gaze. 'One of them looks familiar.' I scratch my head, dislodging my thoughts. 'He is a policeman, he's the one who arrested Granny Bagpuss.'

'I like Granny Bagpuss.'

'What do you mean, you like her?'

'I fancy her. I might even ask her out.'

'But you're a giraffe. A dead one. And she's an old woman. Serving a life sentence for footwear theft. It's hardly the basis for a stable long-term relationship.'

'Who asked you anyway?'

'No one,' I say, taken aback. 'But Jim, I care about you. You're my friend. Whether you like it or not. And I don't want to see you get hurt.' I narrow my eyes. 'Are you really thinking of asking her out?'

He laughs.

'You were joking, weren't you.'

'Of course I was joking. As if I would ask out an old woman. Mind you,' he adds, 'I would fuck her.'

'Well, obviously.'

The barman puts the second of two pints on the counter, more commonly known as the bar. When the barman asks Jim for five pounds, he just looks at me.

'Don't look at me, Jim. I didn't bring my wallet.'

'I can't pay for it.'

I bite my lip. 'Haven't you got anything on you at all?'

Jim steps away from the bar, and spins round. 'Count the pockets,' he says playfully.

'If you were a ghost kangaroo, we'd be all right.' I pat the sides of my trousers, feign a look of surprise, pull out my wallet. 'Oh.'

Jim shakes his head. 'Tight git.'

'You're the tight one. You wouldn't even let me have some of your soup.'

'What soup?'

'The garlic soup.'

'What garlic soup?'

'The tinned garlic soup.'

'What tinned garlic soup?'

'The soup, the tinned garlic soup.'

'What soup the soup the tinned garlic soup?'

I give up. No point arguing with him, not when he's like this. Admitting defeat, I take a neatly folded note from my wallet and hand it to the barman, who screws it into a ball, unscrews it and drops it into the till.

Jim holds up his pint. 'Cheers.'

I perform what is known as a double take. 'Did you just hold up your pint?'

He nods.

'Jim, forgive me for stating the obvious, but you're a giraffe. Now don't get me wrong. I don't mean to put you down. What you lack in the fingers and thumbs department you more than make up for in neck length. But as the proud owner of four cloven hoofs, you do not possess the ability to hold a pint of beer.'

'So what do you want me to do, slurp it through a straw?'

'Not in this place. Anyhow, that's beside the point. The point, Jim, is that you, a four-legged mammal, held up a pint glass. And I would like to know how you did it.'

'It's easy when you've got the know-how.'

'And?'

'A velcro adaptor.'

'You come here a lot, don't you.'

He nods. 'I'm one of the regulars.'

'Do they not notice that you're a ghost giraffe?'

'Look around you,' Jim says. 'They're pissed out of their heads.'

'Surely the barman became suspicious when you asked him for the adaptor.'

'I told him I'm disabled.' He grins. 'You can get away with anything if you tell people you're disabled.'

'Example?'

He thinks for a moment, then says: 'Eating with your mouth open.'

'Pathetic. Anyway, cheers.' I chink my pint glass against his pint glass. It makes a satisfying sound, and gives me a chance to get a proper look at that adaptor. It consists of a velcro strap strapped around his ankle wrist and a small square of velcro glued to the glass. 'So what do we do now?'

He wipes beer foam from his top lip. 'Drink.'

'Then what?'

'Vomit. Lose your front-door key. And collapse in the gutter.'

'So this is what I've been missing.'

'We could talk to some girls.'

'Then why don't we?'

'There aren't any girls in here. Plenty of old men, but no girls.'

'I saw a prostitute in the car park.'

'Hang on though, Spec. You're married. What do you want to talk to girls for?'

'Um, shall we sit down?' I lead him into a dark, smoky corner, where we each pull up a cracked leather chair and make ourselves at home, Jim gazing into space, me thinking about grim, bloody death.

'Spec?'

I snap out of my reverie to find my entire field of vision filled with Jim.

'Spec, what's up?'

'Don't worry about me. I'm just dying, that's all. Jim, I'm going to come clean. You remember when I told you that my wife is sunbathing at her mother's house. And that her mother has a new sunbed. Which she won. In the pizza-relief-fund raffle. Jim. Jim, are you awake?'

'Eh?' He lifts his head from the table, wiping saliva from his chin.

'Are you tired, Jim?'

'Bored.'

'I thought you liked going to the pub.'

'Not with you.'

'Well, did you hear what I just said, about coming clean?'

'No.'

I scratch my left ear. 'You remember back at my house, early this morning. The pizza and the beer, and the pornographic magazines.'

He nods.

'The truth is, Jim, I bought those items for you.'

'For me?'

'Well—'

His head lights up, like a giraffe-head-shaped light bulb.

'Well, yes,' I say, somewhat relieved. 'I know how much you like pizza. And beer. And how dirty you are. Mentally, I mean. Well, when I say mentally, I mean morally. Morally corrupt. What I mean is, I know how you appreciate erotic photography.'

'For me?'

'For you, yes. I bought it all for you, as a present. Because you, Jim, are my best friend. And I like you.'

'Spec, if you ever need me to do anything for you, anything at all, just ask.'

'Why, thank you, Jim, I shall.'

'I won't do it, of course.'

'Oh.'

'Be too busy hoofing off over them porn mags, or downing them beers.'

'Fair enough.'

'Now, what's all this about dying?'

'Yes. The doctor said—'

'You're going to choke on your own dandruff.'

'Jim, this is serious.'

'You didn't believe all that bollocks about shagging the wife, did you? I made all that up, Spec. For a laugh.'

'You made it up?'

He blows beer froth out through his nostrils.

'Was that a no, or a yes?'

'Left nostril for no, right nostril for I don't know.'

'Well, either way. I mean, either nostril. By some unlikely coincidence. Or mammalian intuition. You hit the coffin nail right on the head.' I drink some beer, gulp gulp gulp. 'Jim, just before I left the hospital, Doctor Giraffe told me that I will die unless I explore my sexuality.'

'So why are you telling me?'

'I don't know the first thing about sex. I know where to put it, and where to get it tested, but that's about it.'

'And what makes you think I know anything about it?'

How can I put this, I ask myself, without causing offence? 'You're a pervert.'

'And?'

'You were brought up in the toughest part of the jungle, the east side, so you're obviously very worldly.'

'That's just fighting and stuff. Mind you, the way I do it, sex is a bit like fighting. There's no technique to it. Just wait till she's in a good mood, bend her over the washing machine and hop on.'

'But Doctor Giraffe was very specific. He said that I should perform every sex act in the lovemaker's lexicon,' I explain. He looks blank, so I add: 'You don't even know what that is, do you?'

'I do.' He thinks for a bit, then says: 'It's a shape.'

'A shape?'

'You know, like triangles and stuff. Lovemaker's triangle, lovemaker's square, lovemaker's lexicon.'

'You're not thinking of hexagon, by any chance, are you?'

He doesn't say anything. For one who is wrong at least twenty times a day, you would think that Jim would be used to it by now.

'Jim, a lexicon is a dictionary.'

'Eh?'

'Though not a real dictionary in this case. Doctor Giraffe was speaking metaphorically.'

'Has it got pictures?'

'How can it, if it doesn't exist?'

'They're probably just drawings anyway. That sort of book never has good pictures.'

'Jim, read my lips. It. Does. Not. Ex. Ist.'

'I thought you said this man was a professional?'

'He was. And still is, no doubt. Jim, do you remember when we talked about metaphor? The lovemaker's lexicon,' I explain, 'is a metaphor for all the commonly practised sexual acts.'

He nods.

'All I want you to do, Jim, is tell me what those sexual acts might involve.'

'Oh.' He buys himself another drink— with my money, of course— and brings it back to the table. 'You start off with normal stuff. Vaginal, oral and, um, anal. And bondage. After that, it all gets a bit kinky.'

I sink into my sweatshirt, which sinks beneath the table, taking me and my embarrassment with it. 'Jim, my wife would never let me do any of those things. Maybe the first one. And the second, if it were her birthday. But the others. She would find them disgusting.'

'Are you sure about that?'

My head is suddenly filled with memories, snippets of conversation. The horse, the dildo. I'm not sure about anything any more. 'All right,' I concede, 'perhaps she would do them. But I wouldn't want her to do them. Which amounts to the same thing.'

'Spec, do you remember what we said outside, about pros-titutes?'

'Remind me.'

'You told me that you would rather die than have sex with a prostitute. And I said that we would soon see about that. I said it mysteriously, before passing even more mysteriously through the closed pub door.'

'You don't miss a trick.'

'A magic trick,' he says laterally. 'The hoof is quicker than the eye.'

'Never mind all that. You think I should cheat on my wife, and perform these acts with a prostitute.'

He nods.

'But Jim, that would be immoral.'

Jim folds his front legs across his chest as you or I might fold your or my arms. 'On the contrary, you'd be doing it for her.'

'Well, if you put it like that. There was a prostitute in the car park.'

Jim shakes his head. 'You see that man over there?'

'With the chequered suit?'

'That's Mr Bingo, the, um—' Jim rubs his chin with his hoof, then smiles a crafty giraffe smile. 'The ringmaster, from the travelling suburban circus.'

'Oh, I love the travelling suburban circus,' I say cheerfully, as I follow Jim into an even darker corner of the Bad Leg.

'May we join you?'

'Jim, sit down.' For a man who dresses like a homosexual, Mr Bingo speaks with tremendous authority.

'This is Scott, a friend of mine.'

'I'm a very big fan of your work,' I say, my voice swelling with admiration.

Mr Bingo nods. 'Is that right.'

'Particularly when it involves animals.'

'If you lay one finger on my girls, you lose a kneecap.'

'Spec,' Jim says in a loud whisper, 'Mr Bingo is a pimp.'

'But you said—'

'Forgive my four-eyed friend. He mistook you for someone else.'

Mr Bingo straightens his tie, nods. 'Gentlemen, allow me to introduce my business partner, Ape Hands.' A broad figure steps out of the gloom and takes a seat at Mr Bingo's side. He rolls back his shirtsleeves to reveal thick arms coated in thick black hair. 'Ape Hands does all the monkey work, while I sit back, like this,' Mr Bingo says, sitting back, 'and smoke a cigar.'

Ape Hands takes a cigar from his suit pocket, lights it, and hands it to Mr Bingo.

'My friend here is interested in hiring one of your girls,' Jim says.

'Is that right,' Mr Bingo says, eyeing me curiously. 'Is that right.'

I nod my head. Actually, I shake it, but it might as well be a nod for all the good it does.

Mr Bingo leads the three of us up a narrow flight of stairs to a small back bedroom, lit by a single red light bulb. 'This is Karen Ding, my favourite of all my girls.'

Being more frightened than I have ever been in my entire life, I say the first thing that comes into my head, the only thing that comes into my head, a line, I think, from a film. 'Is she clean?'

Mr Bingo looks at me in disbelief. Ape Hands steps forward, cracking his knuckles, but Mr Bingo holds him back. 'Of course she's clean,' Mr Bingo says. 'All my girls are clean. You know why? Because they're pure. Pure as the driven snow. Ape Hands and I are puritans, ain't that right, Ape Hands.'

Ape Hands nods.

'Karen is the purest of all my girls. Stand up, Karen, let's get a look at you.'

She stands up, performs a twirl. Small, about twenty I would guess, red T-shirt, denim shorts, long blonde hair.

'Say hello to Scott, Karen,' Mr Bingo tells her.

'Hello, Scott,' Karen says. But she doesn't say it to me, she says it to Mr Bingo.

'Scott is going to be spending a little time with you, ain't that right, Scott.'

I nod apologetically.

Nobody says anything after that. I pull out my wallet, but I'm running out of money. I doubt I'd be able to perform the entire lexicon for three pounds fifty.

Mr Bingo gestures for me to put my wallet away. 'Jim and I go way back. Jimbo, this is for that favour you done me back in eighty-six, with that troupe of dancing girls.'

Jim nods. What a dark horse he is. Well, a dark giraffe.

With the door closed, Karen and I are able to relax. Well, not relax exactly. I pace the room, while Karen perches herself on a corner of the mattress, biting her fingernails. Peering through the keyhole, I can see Ape Hands stood midway across the landing, his legs apart, his hands behind his back. When I look back, Karen has got up from the bed and is in the process of pulling off her T-shirt.

'Karen, do you mind if we leave our clothes on?'

'Mr Bingo insists that I satisfy every customer.'

'And what happens if you don't?'

'He beats me,' Karen says. 'With a chair.'

'Oh. Karen, there is something I have to tell you, something which you may find a little shocking.' I pause, adding dramatic tension. 'Karen, I'm married. I'm a married man.'

She nods. 'But what did you want to tell me?'

'That's it.'

'That you're a married man?' She giggles. 'They all are, that's why they come here.'

'No, you've got it all wrong.' I choose my next words very carefully, not wanting to cause any undue alarm. 'Karen, I am suffering from an unusual medical condition.'

'I have condoms.'

'Not that sort of medical condition. I have to perform every sex act in the lovemaker's lexicon—'

'We could do them here first, then go there another time.'

'It's a metaphor, Karen, not a nightclub.'

'Is there a difference?'

Whatever else you might say about her, Karen is not particularly bright. This explains why she is a prostitute, and I am Head Script Writer for a national television channel. Also, Karen has the better legs. 'What if we just don't do it at all? No one will ever know. You could make some funny noises, then I could zip up my trousers and walk out, smoking a cigarette.'

'Mr Bingo always has Ape Hands look me over.' She hangs her head, embarrassed, and I begin to wonder if she might be in the wrong profession. 'He sniffs my vagina, and if it doesn't smell funny, Mr Bingo beats me.'

'I thought he said Ape Hands does the monkey work?'

'Beating girls isn't monkey work, it's precision work. That's what he always tells me anyway. Me, I don't even know what it means.'

'You don't know what what means?'

'Precision.'

It is precisely at this point that Jim's head appears in the floor, rising up through the threadbare carpet. 'Sorry, you weren't meant to see me. I was trying to come up under Karen's skirt.'

'Karen isn't wearing a skirt,' I say, with reference to her denim shorts.

'She shouldn't be wearing anything by now, Spec. Or did you do it already, and she got dressed again?'

'Karen,' I say, seating myself at the end of the bed, 'I think you deserve an explanation. You see, Jim here is a ghost, which is why he is able to poke his head through the floor. And if you were wondering why he looks like a giraffe—'

'No need to explain,' Karen says. 'Mr Bingo gives me drugs.'

'Get on with it, Spec, I'm getting neckache.'

'Jim, Karen and I have decided not to do it. We barely know each other for one thing, and—'

'Spec, look at her. Just look at her.'

I do. She is sat beside me on the bed, her T-shirt off, her breasts as ripe as two ripe fruits. 'As I was saying, Karen and I have decided not to do it, but we are worried that Mr Bingo may take offence. And kill us.'

'I have an idea,' Karen says. 'What if the ghost giraffe—'

'I do have a name, you know.'

'What if Jim, the ghost giraffe, licks me out. His bad breath will make my vagina smell, and Mr Bingo will think that you and I have had sex.'

'Bollocks. What makes you think I've got bad breath? Unless you've got telescopic nostrils.'

'Animals always have bad breath,' Karen says. 'My mum told me. She works at the zoo.'

'Karen didn't mean to be personal,' I say in the prostitute's defence. 'But she does have a point, Jim. You do suffer from halitosis.'

'Bollocks. I live on a diet of leaves. Fresh ones. From the very tops of the trees.'

'And beer,' I correct. 'And pizza, and peanuts, and garlic soup. And that's just for breakfast.'

'It's the weekend, Spec. Everyone pigs out at the weekend.'

'Shush! What was that noise?'

Karen laughs. 'That was just Ape Hands cracking his knuckles. He hasn't killed anyone all week, and today is his birthday.'

'Then we had better get on with it. Jim,' I say decisively, 'poke out your tongue. Karen, step out of your clothes and squat over the ghostly head. I shall wait over here.' I stand in the corner, facing the wall. There then follows a series of slurping noises and an unnerving wailing sound, the sound of a young woman achieving orgasm.

'Hold on, Spec. I've just remembered something.'

'What?'

'Just before I poked my head through the ceiling, me and Mr Bingo were having a chat. I complimented him on his nice teeth, saying how nice they are, and he let me try some of his mouthwash. And very tasty it was too.'

'So what are you saying?'

'My breath doesn't smell. It won't make Karen's vagina smell, and the plan won't work.'

'Karen, I think you should get dressed.'

'It was quality stuff,' Jim says, apparently to himself. 'He has it imported. From abroad.'

'Karen, are you decent?'

'Yes,' she says. 'You can look now.'

I turn round. Oh. 'You might at least close your legs.' I grab her clothes from the carpet and drop them into her lap. 'Karen, Jim and I are trying to help you, and all you can do is flash your internal workings. And as for you, Jim. How odd that you didn't remember about the mouthwash until after you had licked Karen's vagina.'

He grins. 'Funny, that.'

'So now what are we going to do?'

Jim chews his lower lip for a moment, chewing it over. 'Does that window open?'

'Yes,' Karen says. 'I open it when I have sex with fat people.'

'Open it.' Jim disappears back into the carpet, then floats up outside the window, on the other side of the glass.

'Karen, where are you going?'

'Outside,' Karen says, climbing out through the window. 'Jim is rescuing us.'

Jim nods. 'Let me take you away from all this.'

'Wait,' I exclaim, hopping on to the bed, 'I'm coming too.'

'There's no room,' Jim says.

'What do you mean, there's no room?'

'I'm a giraffe, not a double-decker bus.'

'Jim, if you don't let me on—'

He sighs a heavy spectral sigh. 'If you're getting on, get on. And get on with it. I'm getting itchy wings.'

'You haven't got any wings,' I say as I climb aboard.

Karen giggles. 'He has. Silver ones, like an angel.'

He does have wings, one sticking out on either side of his flank. 'You'll be playing the harp next,' I joke.

As the giraffe rises into the air, I put my arms around the

prostitute as though riding pillion on a motorcycle, with Jim as the motorcycle and the prostitute as the motorcycle driver, or rider.

'Yippee,' Karen cries.

'Yes,' I state with equal enthusiasm. 'Yippee.'

Looking down, we can see suburbia fading from sight as we rise up into the clouds, the ghost giraffe beating its angelic—

'Jim, these are plastic.' I reach down and remove the wings. 'Where did you get them?'

'I nicked them off some girl. She was coming home from a party, off her tits on cocaine.'

'Off her what?'

'Tits. On cocaine.'

'And you stole her angel wings. Is there any innocence left in the world, I wonder.'

Right on cue, Karen claps her hands and says: 'Can we go to the seaside? Please, Jim, can we?'

Jim shakes his head. 'I haven't got any trunks.'

'Do they make trunks in your size? Not that it matters. You go around naked all day. Why would you need trunks?'

'I might fancy a swim.'

'And?'

He doesn't answer at first, he's concentrating on a difficult bit of flying. 'If I swim naked, my bollocks bob about, and it scares the children.'

'I'm not surprised.'

'And what about—' He ducks his head, to avoid a low-flying hot-air balloon. 'What about jellyfish? I might get stung by a jellyfish, right on the end of my knob.'

'Serves you right,' I say, getting into the holiday spirit.

The whole journey is like that, with Jim and I sharing

hilarious banter. Every few minutes, Karen will ask Jim if we are nearly there yet, and Jim will throw back his head and laugh. Good, clean fun. You wouldn't think that just twenty minutes ago he had his tongue up her business end.

Eventually, the clouds part like white curtains to reveal a vast expanse of blue, not sky this time but sea. We all cheer as the ghost giraffe descends, slowly at first, then gathering speed, landing with a thud halfway along the deserted prom.

'Come on,' I say, jumping down and helping Karen down, 'let's get some ice cream. Who wants one?'

Jim licks his lips, but Karen doesn't reply, just hangs her head, like a coat hanger.

'Karen, whatever is the matter?'

'If I go back to the Bad Leg, Mr Bingo will beat me.'

'Then stay here, at the seaside. You can find a job. We can help you, can't we, Jim?'

'But I want to go back.'

'Whatever for?'

'If I go back, Mr Bingo will beat me.'

I pull a face. 'Do you like to be beaten, Karen?'

She nods.

'Then what are we doing here? Jim, I think you had better take Karen back to the Bad Leg.'

'Don't fly too fast,' Karen says, climbing back aboard the ghost giraffe. 'If we get there really late, he might use the table.'

'All right, but I want to watch. Are you coming with us, Spec?'

The beach is almost deserted, but there is one figure, a woman, lying on her back. Her face is hidden behind sunglasses, but I recognise her as my wife. 'Jim, you two go without me. I have something I have to do.'

'Spec,' Jim says, following my gaze, 'isn't that your missus?'
I nod.

'You should fuck her.'

'That was what I meant, when I said that there is something I have to do.'

'Give it to her from behind, then pull it out and shoot it over her arse.'

'Thank for the advice, Jim, but true love needs no choreographer.'

'And don't put it in till she's nice and wet.'

'Jim, please. I'm nervous enough as it is.'

'Take a chill pill. It's only sex. It's not as if you haven't done it before.'

'Goodbye, Jim.'

'Goodbye, Spec. And good luck.'

I wait for the ghost giraffe and the kinky prostitute to disappear out of sight, then make my way down to the beach. My wife is some way off, and it takes me several minutes to reach her. As my shadow falls across her brown bikini, she pushes her round brown sunglasses up into her straight brown hair, blinks her brown eyes, and says: 'Scott.'

'Continence. I thought you were with your mother.'

'I am with my mother. She wanted to go to the seaside, so we came to the seaside.'

'Where is she now?'

'Back at the bed and breakfast. Last night, we went to the cabaret. They had dancing girls, and it made my mother feel young again, and she danced, and fell over.'

'Continence,' I say, swallowing my pride, 'I want to make love to you. Here, on the beach.' I look around. There is no one around. 'Can I? Can I make love to you? Here. On the beach.'

'Maybe,' Continence says, wriggling her toes at the sun. 'I mean, yes.'

I undo my trousers and drop them to the sand. I wait for my wife to burst out laughing, but she doesn't, so I pull down my boxer shorts and step out of my trousers and boxer shorts and put them in a pile, along with my shoes and socks, my sweatshirt, my T-shirt. And here I am, naked, pale, a bit hairy in the middle.

Continence sits up, smiles. 'My cavalier,' she says, and I am just wondering which of us she is talking to, myself or my penis, when she opens her mouth and closes it over the end.

Rhinoceros Poo

Harry has been my boss ever since I first got into television. It was Harry who gave the green light for what proved to be the Science Fiction Channel's biggest hit of the decade, Space Man In Space. My idea. In Harry Maker's eyes, I can do no wrong.

I cross the open-plan office to my desk, say good morning to my secretary, Ms Moody, put down my bag and switch on my computer. The moment I sit down, Harry comes over, dressed in his attention-seeking silver suit, his hairy belly showing through his see-through silver shirt. It being dress-down Monday, he isn't wearing a tie. 'I hear congratulations are in order,' he says, dropping a plastic folder on to my desk.

'Thanks, Harry.' He's referring to my big news, of which more later.

'No wonder you were so keen to put your all into the new

show. If we get a hit, the annual bonus will be conglomerate.'

I indicate the plastic folder. 'What's this, Harry?'

'That, dear heart, is the new show.'

I look up into Harry's face, to see if he is joking. He isn't. 'But Harry, we haven't had the meeting.'

'What meeting?'

'Well, any meeting. Aren't we going to brainstorm?'

He shakes his head.

'The Scott Spectrum Think Tank,' I say, citing the name of a file on my computer, 'is absolutely brimming with quality programme ideas.'

'Is it?'

I swivel on my swivel chair, pick up the folder, drop it back on to the desk. 'Harry,' I say, but then I don't say anything else.

Harry walks up to my secretary, gestures for her to stand, wheels her swivel chair over to my desk and sits down. 'Scott, Space Man In Space was a brilliant idea, brilliant. So brilliant, in fact, that I often wonder why I didn't think of it myself. But I didn't. And you did. And why? Because you're brilliant.'

'Why, thank you, Harry.'

He rubs his nostril, sniffs. 'You are brilliant, Scott, brilliant.' Over his shoulder, I watch Ms Moody shake her head several times. She's leaning against the filing cabinet, filing her nails.

'But Harry, if I'm so brilliant, why haven't I been consulted on the new show?'

'Well, maybe you're a little too brilliant.'

'How can I be too brilliant?'

He pauses again, rubs his nose again, laughs. 'If we knew how you did it, Scott, we would all be doing it.'

'That wasn't what I meant. I simply meant that there is no such thing as too brilliant. The more brilliant I am, the more brilliant my ideas. And the more valuable my input.'

'In theory, yes. In practice, no.'

'Well, I still think I should have been consulted.'

Harry swivels authoritatively in my secretary's swivel chair, pauses, pauses again, and says: 'Scott, a few months ago, I had a peek at the Scott Spectrum Think Tank.' He reaches into his attention-seeking silver suit and pulls out a folded sheet of computer printer paper. He unfolds it, clears his throat, reads. 'Giraffe Killer. Catch The Giraffe. Death To The Giraffe. Tall, Yellow And Stupid. Chop His Legs Off. Saw His Legs Off. While He Is Running Along.' He refolds the sheet of computer printer paper and drops it into the rubbish bin. 'So you see. You were consulted. In a sense.'

'But they were just notes. Half-formed ideas.'

Harry exercises his facial muscles, then says: 'Scott. The problem with your ideas is not that they are half formed, the problem with your ideas is that they are crap.'

'Does this mean I'm out of a job?'

He shakes his head. 'You are still brilliant, dear heart. And I want you to work on the show.' He pauses. 'This show.'

I look down at the plastic folder. 'This show, in this folder.'

He nods.

I pick up the folder, open it, take out a single sheet of computer printer paper, read. 'Real-life documentary. Hidden camera. Place large piece of wood on a street corner and watch as working-class people try to "shift" it.'

Ms Moody is a good secretary, but she does like to do things her way. She takes Thursdays and Fridays off, and Wednesday afternoons, and she never, ever speaks to me before half past eleven. 'I heard you have some big news,' she says to me at thirty-one minutes past eleven.

'My wife and I are having a baby.'

'Let me just finish typing this sentence, then I can congratulate you properly.' Ms Moody finishes typing a very long sentence. I step forward, expecting a hug or a kiss on the cheek or at least a handshake, but all she does is look me up and down and says: 'Are you adopting?'

I shake my head.

'Artificial insemination?'

I swivel uncomfortably. 'We are making it ourselves.'

'Oh. And what are you going to call it?'

'My wife has chosen the girl name, Eclair, and I have chosen the boy name.'

'Which is?'

'Turbo.'

'Turbo,' Ms Moody says, trying it on for size. 'You're going to call it Turbo.'

'If it's a boy.'

Ms Moody shakes her head. 'It doesn't work.'

'We chose a name each.'

'Yes, but your wife chose a nice name.'

'Turbo is a nice name.'

'For a car, Scott. Or part of one. The part that makes it go really fast. But not for a baby.'

'That is neither here nor there. Turbo is our baby, and we will call it whatever we like.'

'Over my dead body.'

'Excuse me?'

Ms Moody folds her arms. 'If you call your baby Turbo, I am taking you to court.'

'Are you serious?'

She nods.

'This is ludicrous. How can you take me to court on your wages? Not that you would be earning any wages. Harry and I are like that.' I twist two of my fingers together, to illustrate what Harry and I are like.

Ms Moody looks at me, shakes her head, then looks at me again. 'You were joking, weren't you? About calling your baby Turbo.'

'Um. Yes.'

'What kind of idiot would call their baby Turbo?'

'Not me.'

'Talking of idiocy,' Ms Moody says, 'did you see the outline for the new show? Anyone who agrees to work on a show like that needs their head examining.'

An hour later, I storm into Harry Maker's office, all guns blazing. I knock first of course. After all, he is Harry Maker.

'Scott,' he says, 'take a seat.'

I remain standing.

The telephone rings. Harry picks it up and begins a lengthy conversation with his partner, Doctor Bang, author of the best-selling popular-science book Why Blood Is Sticky. I sit down.

'Scott,' Harry says, more than twenty minutes later. 'And how, dear heart, are you?'

'Fine. Well, not fine exactly. Not at all fine, in fact. I have identified a problem with the new show.'

'I'm listening.'

I reach into the back pocket of my graph-paper trousers and pull out a folded sheet of computer printer paper. I unfold it, clear my throat. 'Real-life documentary,' I read. 'Hidden camera. Place large piece of wood on a street corner and watch as working-class people try to "shift" it.'

'And what, dear heart, i

'This is the Science Fic

problem with the new sho

fictional.'

'How do you mean?'

'Science fiction is fiction. Th

'Is it?'

'Well, half of the point.'

'And the other half?'

'I was just coming to that. Wooc   ,, is one of the most unscientific construction materials in the construction industry. Could we not use a piece of plastic? Plastic is scientific. It's made by scientists.'

Harry shakes his head authoritatively. 'Let me tell you something about working-class people, Scott. Working-class people do not "shift" pieces of plastic. I have known working-class people, and I have never known any of them to "shift" pieces of plastic. They have no interest in it.'

'Point taken,' I concede. 'But returning to the fiction element. Could we not use actors? We used actors in Space Man In Space and it worked very well.'

'I don't follow.'

'We lose the real-life angle and opt for a plot-driven approach. Instead of hidden cameras,' I go on, 'we could film the whole show in the studio.'

Harry rubs his chin, nods.

'Also, I wonder if we could lose the working-class people. You know the maxim, Harry. Never work with animals or children. Or working-class people.'

'Are you sure you've got that right?'

I nod.

Harry nods too, though with more authority. 'Some good

one thing that you have forgotten.'

ve I forgotten?'

olders.'

hareholders?'

ll, when I say shareholders perhaps I should say share-
older. There is only one shareholder, and that is my partner,
Doctor Bang.'

'Doctor Bang.'

He nods.

'When did Doctor Bang become a shareholder? The
shareholder?'

'Last weekend. We were on a mini-break in Paris,' Harry
explains, 'and he had me over a barrel.'

'But Harry, you don't even own the Science Fiction
Channel. Never did. You just work here. Like I do. Though
obviously with a lot more stature,' I add respectfully.

'Doctor Bang isn't a real shareholder, dear heart, he's a
virtual shareholder. You know what virtual means, do you
not?'

I do of course, but, not knowing what Harry Maker is
talking about, I shake my head.

'The way it works, dear heart, is this. I have to do exactly
as Doctor Bang tells me,' Harry says. 'Think of it as a bondage
session that extends beyond my personal life and into my
professional life. And into yours.'

I nod, though I still don't know what he is talking about.

'So you see,' Harry says, 'the only way to change the new
show is to speak with Doctor Bang.' He leans back in his
chair, his silver leather shoes up on the desk.

I lean back in my chair and put my shoes up on the desk
too, though only in my head. 'Fine. Call him.'

Harry picks up the telephone, presses some buttons, holds

the receiver to his ear just long enough to verify that it is ringing, then passes the receiver across the desk to me.

'Doctor Bang,' I say, when he picks up. 'This is Scott Spectrum, from the Science Fiction Channel.'

'Scott,' he says, thinking aloud. 'Weren't you the chap who photocopied his breasts at the office party?'

'That was my secretary, Ms Moody,' I clarify. 'And the breasts were both hers.'

'Forgive me. Now, what can I do for you?'

'I wanted to discuss the new show.'

'Then you should talk to Harry Maker, your boss.'

'I did,' I say patiently. 'Harry says that I should talk to you.'

'Then Harry Maker knows what is good for him. Why not come round for dinner?' Doctor Bang says. 'You could bring your wife. Or leave her at home, if you prefer. Either way, tonight, my house, at ten.'

Satisfied, I return to my desk. As I sit down, my secretary Ms Moody calls me over. I ask her to come over here but she tells me that she is tired. 'I hope you gave him what for,' she says as I approach her desk.

'Yes. Well, as good as.'

'You had a call from a Mr Twenty.'

'Vic, my best friend. Did he leave a message?' Vic is notoriously difficult to get hold of, not because he leads a full life but because he is a computer programmer, and is always too busy computer programming to answer the telephone.

'He said to tell you that it is ready.'

'Good. Give Jim a call, tell him to meet me at my house. I have a surprise for him.'

Although my wife is pregnant, she is only a bit pregnant and is still able to do wife things such as wash the pots and pans: 'Hello,' she says, washing the pans and pots. 'Did you have a good day?'

I pretend not to hear her and creep up behind her and hug her from behind, pretending to think that I am surprising her.

'You and your joke. It always reminds me of your friend, Vic. And not in a good way.'

She is referring of course to Vic's joke, which involves waving at you from afar, then walking towards you and waving again, right up close to your face.

'Talking of Vic, I have to go to his house, with Jim.'

'What about dinner?' Continence says, drying her hands.

'We have been invited to Bang House, to dine with Harry Maker and Doctor Bang.'

'Then I have cooked all of this food for nothing?'

'Yes,' I state logically.

Continence removes her apron and leaves the room.

In the past, Jim Giraffe treated me like dirt. Now that I have proved my masculinity by ejaculating into my wife, he has found new respect for me. Not only does he enter the house via the front door rather than the bedroom wardrobe, he has also stopped calling me Spec.

'Scott,' Jim says, not calling me Spec.

'Jim, come in.'

'Is Continence here?'

'No,' I reply. 'She popped upstairs to get something, or something.'

'So what's all this about?'

'Go through to the lounge,' I tell him. 'Would you like a cup of tea?'

He nods.

'Milk?'

'Yes please, Spec.'

'Sugar?'

'Fifteen lumps.'

I make the teas, then carry them through to the lounge, where the ghost giraffe is stretched out along the sofa, his long legs entangled in a ghost giraffe leg knot.

'So how are you enjoying parenthood?'

'I'm not a parent yet,' I say, climbing aboard my high-tech armchair. 'We have only been pregnant for two weeks.'

'How long does it take, Spec? For the baby to come out?'

'Nine months.'

He inverts his nose. 'I thought it was nine days, something like that.'

'Nine days?'

'Well,' he says, recoiling from my mocking tone. 'Nine weeks, then.'

'Didn't you study biology at school, Jim?'

'The only sex education we were given in the jungle,' Jim says, 'was take her from behind, then run away.'

'I never knew you were such a romantic.'

'You have to be practical,' Jim says, slurping his tea. 'It's a jungle out there.'

I nod. 'Jim, there is something I have been wanting to tell you. I haven't always treated you very well, have I?'

'Why should you?' Jim says modestly. 'What have I ever done for you?'

I adjust my position. 'Rather a lot, as it happens. You have brought me out of my shell, for one thing. I was able to look Harry Maker in the eye today and criticise his new television show.'

'Because of me?'

'Well, not just because of you, Jim. It was partly to do with my secretary, Ms Moody, belittling me. I said to myself, what would Jim do if he were belittled?'

'Tell the belittler to kiss my tail.'

'Exactly. Which is what I did, in a sense. And as a thank you, I would like to take you to Vic Twenty's house so that you can play a game on his computer.'

'I don't know what to say.'

'Just drink up your tea, and we'll get going.'

'I can't drink it,' Jim says, untangling his legs. 'I'm too excited.'

'Then leave it. I will leave mine, too, so that you don't feel guilty. Come on,' I say, looking at my high-tech watch, 'Vic is picking us up in his car, and he'll be here any minute. I hope we can all fit. It's only a hatchback, and you're a giraffe.'

'Can I bring a friend?'

'What friend?'

'Barry.'

'This isn't the ghost elephant you told me about, is it?'

'Rhinoceros.'

I sigh. 'If you must. But just him, nobody else.' I look at my high-tech watch again. 'How quickly can he get here?'

'He's here already, Spec. He lives in the kitchen, under the sink.'

'Terrific. How many other dead animals do I share my house with?'

'Hardly any.'

I follow Jim to the kitchen. 'I should never have agreed to this. If he's really heavy, he'll have to pay some petrol money.'

As I open the under-the-sink cupboard door, the rhinoceros

looks up at me, blinking his great grey eyes. 'Oh,' he says. 'I was asleep.'

Jim bends his neck, bringing his face face to face with the rhinoceros face. 'Barry, this is Scott. Scott, this is Barry, the phosphorous rhinoceros.'

'Hello, Barry.'

'Goodbye,' Barry says. 'I mean, hello.'

'Barry isn't very clever,' Jim says. 'He lives under the sink,' he adds, and I'm not sure if this is intended as an explanation or as an example.

'What day is it?'

'I don't know, Barry. Scott, what day is it?'

'Monday,' I tell them.

Barry nods twice, which takes some time as he nods it very slowly. 'So what does that mean?'

Jim looks at me.

'It depends on whether or not you have a job, I suppose.'

'He does have a job,' Jim says.

I laugh. 'Let me guess. He's a chartered accountant.'

'Nice try, Spec. He works at the public toilets, eating poo.'

'That was my second guess.'

Jim looks at the phosphorous rhinoceros, smiles. 'Barry, do you want to come out with us?'

'Not bowling again. I hate bowling. Doing a poo and rolling it down that wood thing.'

'He did it wrong,' Jim tells me in an aside.

Barry looks up. 'What was that? Did you just call me a sore loser? I'm not a sore loser.'

'You didn't even lose, Barry. Your poo was so big, you got a strike every time.'

'Then why did I get beaten up?'

'You did a poo,' Jim says. 'What did you expect?'

'I'm a rhinoceros,' Barry says. 'What did they expect?'

Vic arrives on time, to the exact second. After a few brief introductions, we get down to the serious business of organising the seating arrangements. Being a computer programmer, Vic has excellent problem-solving skills. Unfortunately, they are primarily suited to abstract mathematical problems, rather than the more day-to-day problem of squeezing a rhinoceros and a giraffe into a hatchback.

'Where are we going?' Barry says as Vic and I push him into the front passenger seat.

'To my house,' Vic tells him.

'No, I mean before that.'

'I have to get some petrol,' Vic says.

'No, I mean before that. Where are we going now?'

'He means the car,' Jim says. 'We're getting into the car.'

'What car?'

Vic and I shake our heads. This could get tiresome.

'It's no good,' Vic says, 'he will have to go in the back.'

'Then can I go in the front?' Jim says enthusiastically. 'You can open the sunroof.'

'What a good idea,' Vic says. 'You can poke your head out, and keep an eye out for traffic jams. Scott, you will have to go in the back, with the rhinoceros.'

I slap myself on the forehead, expressing my disdain. 'And what if he does a poo?'

'We could put some sheets down,' Vic says.

'I won't do one anyway,' Barry says, climbing on to the back seat. 'I just did eight, in the flowers.'

* * *

'Why are the trees running away?' Barry says, looking out of the window.

'Because you're evil,' Jim says, his voice emanating from on high.

Barry blinks his eyes, and a tear emerges, dropping on to the car-floor carpet.

I poke my head out of the window and look up at the ghost giraffe's ghost head. 'Jim,' I plead, 'don't confuse him. He's confused enough as it is.'

'Am I?' Barry says. 'I didn't even know.'

'Barry,' I say kindly, 'the trees aren't running away, we're driving past them, in Vic's car.'

'I thought we were under the sink.'

Vic lives in his mum's house, in the upstairs back bedroom in which he spent his childhood. Being a computer programmer, instead of a loving wife, he has a loving mum and a top-of-the-range personal computer. He tells us to take a seat, but there is only one seat, so he clears the bed of computer programming books and we sit on the bed, me at the pillow end, Jim in the middle, then Barry, staring up at the ceiling.

'What is he looking for, Jim?'

'Pipes,' Jim says. 'He thinks we're under the sink.'

'Barry, this is Vic's bedroom.'

'Is it?' Barry says. 'I didn't even know.'

I ask Barry if he has ever played a computer game.

'Yes. I mean, no. I mean, I don't know.'

Vic has the computer booted up now, and is entering a series of commands. Barry is watching Vic's fingers. 'Look at the screen,' I tell him.

'What screen?'

Vic taps the side of the screen. 'This is the screen, here.'

'In that box, Barry,' I add, 'is Vic's entire life.'

'Is it? How sad.'

Jim laughs. 'Maybe Barry isn't so stupid after all.'

'I was talking metaphorically,' I say in Vic's defence.

'Even so,' Jim says.

The computer screen clears, and some words appear. Jim Giraffe, it says. Programmed by Vic Twenty. Concept by Scott Spectrum. Jim is looking at the screen, but it doesn't seem to register. His face is blank, expectant. Vic presses a button and the screen clears again and a computerised giraffe appears. Jim moves his head closer, squinting at the computerised giraffe. 'That's me.'

Vic nods.

'You've put me in a computer game.'

'What do you think of that?' I say, my arms around Jim's shoulders.

He chews his lip. 'Why am I so small?'

'We had to make you small so that you would fit on the screen.'

He moves even closer, his nose touching the glass, and studies the computerised giraffe carefully. 'How did—' He stops, shakes his head. 'How did—'

I adjust my spectacles. 'Vic wrote a computer program. Do you remember when you got upset because I said that there weren't any computer games with giraffes in them? Well, Jim, you have done a lot for me over the past few months, and I wanted to repay you. I thought, what do you give to the ghost giraffe who has everything? Well, the ghost giraffe who has nothing. But who doesn't need anything. Anyhow, this is what we came up with. Vic did all the difficult work, didn't you, Vic.'

Jim looks at Vic and says: 'You put me in a computer game!'

Vic nods, smiles.

Jim takes a deep breath. 'This is the best thing I have ever seen.'

'You haven't seen anything yet,' Vic says coolly. 'Watch this.' He picks up the joystick, makes himself comfortable, and presses the fire button. Suddenly, a monster runs on to the screen, and Jim— not the computerised Jim, the real Jim— jumps almost out of his skin.

'Steady,' I say reassuringly. 'It's only a game.'

'Is that one of the monsters you were telling me about?'

'Yes,' I confirm. 'But don't worry. Vic knows what to do, don't you, Vic.'

Vic doesn't say anything. He waits for the monster to run towards the computerised giraffe, then, at the optimum moment, presses the joystick fire button, causing the computerised giraffe to leap across the screen and hoof the monster in the head.

Jim's eyes light up. 'I did it. I killed the monster.'

'With a little help from Vic,' I add.

'Let me have a go.'

Vic passes the joystick to me, and I hold it still so that Jim can move the plastic joystick with his teeth. Another monster appears, and Jim wiggles the joystick frantically, and the computerised giraffe runs into it, and dies.

Jim looks devastated.

I grab him by the shoulder and give him a shake. 'Jim, what's wrong? It's only a game, Jim.'

'But we can't play it any more, Spec. If the giraffe is dead, it's just monsters. I've ruined it. I've ruined the game.' He looks at me. 'And you didn't even get a go.'

I cannot help but laugh. 'Oh, Jim. We can play it all over

again, from the beginning. Vic, show him how to restart the game.'

Vic presses some keys and the game restarts.

'I don't understand.'

Vic and I exchange looks. How to explain. 'Jim,' I say, 'do you remember how you died, and then you came back, as a ghost?'

He nods.

'It's like that. But, um, different.'

'Can Barry have a go?'

I look at the rhinoceros, who is looking at the ceiling. 'Barry, would you like to play the Jim Giraffe computer game?'

'No. I mean, yes.'

Vic passes him the joystick. He turns it in his big clumsy hands, or feet. 'Is it food? Or poo?'

'Barry doesn't get out much,' Jim says.

'Neither,' Vic explains. 'That is what we call a computer joystick. Look at the screen. This,' he says, pointing, 'is a monster.'

Barry nods.

'When it runs towards you, what I want you to do, Barry, is kill it.'

Barry nods again, but when the monster runs on to the screen he doesn't do anything.

'You have to kill it,' Vic tells him.

'Kill it!' we shout. 'Kill it!'

Barry drops the joystick, runs at the screen and pierces it with his phosphorous rhinoceros nose horn. The screen explodes, spraying the room with plastic and broken glass. 'Did I kill it?'

Vic and I exchange looks. 'Yes,' I say. 'I suppose you did.'

*   *   *

Doctor Bang and Harry Maker live in a big house at the posh end of suburbia. Continence and I dined here once before. Although we had a nice time, Continence didn't want to come on this occasion, so I have brought Jim instead. This is not as odd as it may seem. You see, Doctor Bang and Harry Maker are gay.

When the door opens, Doctor Bang looks right past me and exclaims: 'Jim!'

I give the ghost giraffe a sideways look. 'Do you two know each other?'

'Um—'

'We were at school together,' Doctor Bang says, 'at Beaten.'

As Doctor Bang disappears into the dining room, I stop the ghost giraffe just inside the front door. 'Jim, you went to a public school?'

He shrugs.

'You always told me that you were brought up in the jungle.'

'Not brought up exactly.'

'But you did live there,' I suggest. 'For a while.'

'I spent some time there, yes.'

'You have friends there, and you used to go and stay.'

'It was only once. For a week. On holiday.'

'You told me that you were brought up there. The toughest part of the jungle, you said. The east side, you said.'

He hangs his head, says nothing.

'But how can you have been at school with Doctor Bang? He must be twenty years your senior.'

He shrugs. 'Giraffe years are different.'

I administer a look of great pity, pause for dramatic effect, and wander off up the hall.

*   *   *

Like the rest of the house, the dining room is big and posh. Doctor Bang is sat at the dining table, dressed in an expensive dinner suit. Rather predictably, Harry Maker is wearing a maid's pinny over his, and has been delegated the task of pouring the wine. I too have made an effort, and am sporting my favourite Science Fiction Channel T-shirt, featuring the Science Fiction Channel logo. Jim, on the other hand, is stark naked, but he has cleaned his toenails.

'So, Jim,' Doctor Bang says. 'What have you been up to all these years?' Before Jim has a chance to answer, Doctor Bang looks at me and says: 'Jim was bullied terribly, you know.'

'That explains a lot.'

'They used to call him a nigger, and hang him up by his shoelaces.'

'Nigger?'

'Yes. There weren't many coloured people at Beaten.'

'Coloured people?'

'And being so tall, he stuck out like a sore thumb.'

I nod.

Jim puts his long mouth to my ear and whispers: 'Doctor Bang thinks I'm black.'

'Black?'

'All the boys did. Public schools are like that, Spec. Full of white upper-class gay idiots.'

I nod. 'Hang on, did you just call me Spec? I thought we had stopped all that.'

'We had.'

Doctor Bang takes a sip of his wine. 'Talking of nicknames, do you know what they used to call our Jim?'

'No,' I say. 'Tell me. Please.'

Doctor Bang unfolds an elaborate napkin, spreads it over

his lap and folds his hands in his lap. 'Big Nose. Here he comes, they would say. Here comes Big Nose, the boy with the biggest nose at Beaten.'

'How imaginative.'

'They would turn him upside down,' Doctor Bang says, 'and flush his head down the toilet. Is that not right, Jim?'

Jim says nothing. He isn't enjoying this, not one bit.

'They did it to me once,' Doctor Bang goes on. 'Never again, I said to myself. Never again will I have my head flushed down the toilet. And do you know what? Since that fateful day, not once have I had my head flushed down the toilet.'

'Remarkable.'

'It was the last day of school, you see.'

I nod. Remarkable.

'Enough of that. Not you, Harriet. Continue to polish, until I say stop.' Harry Maker is on his knees, polishing Doctor Bang's shoes. 'Let us change the subject. Sit down, Jim. And you, Scott. Have some wine.'

We do have wine, lots of wine, and a three-course meal, all served up by Harry Maker, or Harriet, as he has become known. Once the plates have been cleared away, Doctor Bang declares that Harriet is to be Harry again, and we retire to the drawing room where Harry removes his pinny and sits with the rest of us in big leather chairs.

'So,' Doctor Bang says, passing round the cigars. 'What was it you wanted to discuss with me, young Scott?'

'The new show, sir.'

He nods. 'Real-Life Wood "Shifters". Hidden camera. Street corner. Wood. It will be presented as a serious scientific study—'

'Science,' Harry says to me with a wink.

'— but with a strong human interest element. Of course,

real-life working-class people are less than interesting, and can be hell to work with, so the working-class people will be played by classically trained actors—'

'Fiction,' Harry says to me with another wink.

'— who will improvise over a basic script. Right,' he says, lighting his cigar, 'now what was it you wanted to say?'

'Um.'

Harry lights his cigar. 'Scott had a number of points. Is that not right, dear heart?'

'I did have.'

'But you do not have them now,' Harry says.

I shake my head, and light my cigar.

Jim is also lighting a cigar, a very long cigar, which seems to be getting longer. It has a message written on it. Doctor Bang is an idiot, the message says. The show will bomb. The Science Fiction Channel will go bankrupt. You will be out of a job. And your wife and child will starve.

'Jim, may I have a word with you, in the hall?'

The ghost giraffe and I smile politely and leave the room.

'Jim, I don't know what to do.'

'You need to come up with an idea, Spec. And it better be good. So good that Harry Maker will tell Doctor Bang to cock off.'

'Ideas don't grow on trees, Jim.'

'What about the Scott Spectrum Think Tank?'

'How do you know about that?'

'You told me about it.'

'Did I?'

'Yes,' Jim says, shaking his head.

'Well, the Scott Spectrum Think Tank is absolutely brimming with quality programme ideas, as always, but Harry has already seen them, you see, and he is not keen.'

'Why not?'

I remove my spectacles, breathe cloud on to them, wipe the cloud on to my Science Fiction Channel T-shirt and replace my spectacles. 'Harry said that the ideas were half formed.'

Jim nods. 'Well, I have an idea. I'm not sure you'll like it, but if you want it, it's yours.'

'Please,' I plead, 'I'm desperate.'

'A variety show. With a difference.'

'And what will this variety show be called?'

The All New
Jim Giraffe
Variety Show

Jim and I have just been for a stroll, to celebrate my last afternoon as a non-parent. On the edge of town, we watched as a
building was demolished by a group of hard-working working-
class men in hard hats. 'I love that moment,' Jim said. 'The
moment just before everything falls apart.' A moment later,
the steel ball tore into the building, knocking its block off.

When I get home, Continence is sat up in bed. Being a
modern woman, she decided to have the baby at home. I
took out a bank loan and used the money to have my high-
tech armchair converted into a high-tech birthing bed. I
intend to repay the loan out of my annual bonus, which, in
the words of Harry Maker, will be conglomerate. Unless the
show is a flop. Which it won't be, of course. Jim is in it,
and Jim is a ghost giraffe.

'Scott,' Continence says as I enter the room, 'will you pass
me the chocolate?'

'Have you been crying?' I ask her as I pass her the chocolate.

She nods. 'I couldn't reach the chocolate.'

I sit on the edge of the bed and feel her bump. 'I can feel it kicking. When will you go into labour?'

'Difficult to say, but Doctor Apple thinks it will be some time during the show.'

The show to which she refers is, of course, the new show, which airs tonight. 'Well, let's hope it happens during the adverts.'

Continence laughs. 'Labour isn't like that. It could go on for several hours.'

'I haven't played a very active role in this pregnancy, have I.'

Continence smoothes her brown nightie over her round bump. 'Your role, Scott, is the role of provider, and you have provided by working on the new show. You bought me this brown maternity nightie—'

'Your favourite colour.'

'— and the chocolate—'

'Ditto.'

'— and you had your high-tech armchair converted into a high-tech birthing bed, so that I can have the baby at home.'

'Talking of which, who is going to perform the delivery?'

'Doctor Apple.'

'With a midwife,' I suggest, 'and a fleet of nurses?'

'No, just Doctor Apple. I want to keep things simple. Oh,' she cries, moving across the bed, 'I can feel it starting to come out.'

'Shall I call an ambulance?'

'No. Call Doctor Apple. Tell him it is starting to come out.'

As I pull my mobile phone from my trouser pocket, it emits a loud ringing sound. 'It's funny when it does that. I wonder who it could be.' I press the talk button and hold the mobile phone to my ear.

It's Harry Maker, calling from Science Fiction Studios in London. 'Scott, get down here. We need input. Your input.'

'I have to go,' I tell Continence, kissing her on the cheek.

'Don't forget to call Doctor Apple,' Continence says. 'Tell him it is starting to come out.'

Security is always high at Science Fiction Studios, but today it is on red alert, and for good reason. The All New Jim Giraffe Variety Show has become the most hyped television show in television history. Tonight's tickets sold out in a record two point five seconds. Several thousand people have gathered outside the building, hoping to catch a glimpse of the up-and-coming television star.

Harry is waiting for me in reception. 'What happened to you? Did they tear you apart, dear heart?'

'You could say that.' I had almost reached the building when somebody recognised me from my publicity photograph and lunged at my floppy blond fringe. I can see the results reflected in the glass doors. My T-shirt is ripped, my spectacles have been knocked askew and my fringe is imprinted with a deep hand-shaped crimp. More interesting, though, are the doors themselves, high-tech stained-glass windows, one in the shape of Space Man, the other in the shape of his arch-enemy, Bug Eye Alien, who, for legal reasons, had to be written out after the first series.

'Have you spoken to Jim today?'

'Yes,' I say casually. 'We went for a stroll, to celebrate my last afternoon as a non-parent.'

'How was he?'

It is then that I notice the look on Harry's face. The look is best described as a look of very real concern, though one may also employ the word chagrin, if only because it is my favourite. 'He seemed fine. A little distracted maybe, but that is only to be expected.'

Harry nods. He is leaning against the high-tech mock-marble reception desk, the longest of its kind in the world. Sat behind it are an improbable eighteen receptionists, three of whom are left-handed.

'Jim has never been on television before,' I explain. 'He is bound to be a little nervous. I know I would be.'

'He seemed distracted, you say?'

'Yes. Why, is he not here?'

'He was here, dear heart. He checked in over an hour ago, hasn't been seen since.'

'Have you tried the bar?'

'I tried every bar, had a glass of whisky in each.'

I scratch my chin. 'And he isn't in his dressing room?'

'That was the first place we looked.'

'Follow me, Harry. I think I know where he is.'

On Jim's dressing-room door there is a big gold star, a symbol of what he is about to become. Harry knocks on the door, then opens it, and we go in. 'You see?'

I survey the room. A crate of champagne, a selection of unfeasibly long neckties, a photograph of some dancing girls, their stockinged legs captured mid kick.

'You see?' Harry says again.

I pause for dramatic effect, then open the door to the wardrobe. 'Jim.'

'Jim,' Harry says, 'you were wanted in make-up over an hour ago. What do you think you are doing?'

'Hiding.'

'But why?'

'I'm scared, Harry. Of the telly.'

'What telly?' Harry Maker looks around the room for a telly.

'The telly. I've never been on telly before, and I'm scared.'

I give Harry a told-you-so look.

'I'm not going on, Harry. I'm staying in here, in the wardrobe. With the knickers and vests and pants.'

'And the T-shirts,' I add, ever the pedant.

'Leave this to me, Scott,' Harry says to me, giving me a leave-this-to-me look. 'Now, Jim. Dear heart. Tell me this. Who is your favourite television star?'

Jim has to think about this. He doesn't watch television very often, and is unsure who his favourite television star is. Or it's something else, he knows who it is but he doesn't want to say.

Harry folds his arms. He isn't about to let this go.

Jim looks at me for a moment, then looks at Harry, at his silver-plated shoes. 'Space Man.'

'Space Man.'

Jim nods his head, says nothing.

Harry looks at me. 'Did you hear that, Scott?'

I did, but I'm not sure that I believe it, that I believe my ears. Jim's favourite television star is Space Man, a character, my character, whom I made up on a bored Sunday morning over corn flakes.

'Now,' Harry says, 'let me ask you. What would have

happened if Space Man had refused to star in that first episode? What if he had hidden in the wardrobe? With the, um. Clothing. What if he had hidden in the wardrobe, what would have happened to the world?'

'Attacked by monsters.'

'Go on.'

'And robots. Intergalactic robots, with bendy robotic arms.'

'Apart from all that,' Harry says patiently. 'What would have happened to television, to entertainment?'

'Oh,' Jim says, catching on. 'There wouldn't be Space Man In Space, and we wouldn't be able to watch it.'

'Precisely.'

Jim wrinkles his snout, nostril by nostril. Steps out of the wardrobe. Sniffs. 'Thank you, Harry. And you, Scott. For everything.'

'Space Man would be proud of you, Jim.'

'Don't overdo it.'

'Sorry.'

Harry looks at his hologram watch. 'You better get down to make-up. Come along, Scott. We shall proceed to the bar. And drink a well-earned drink.'

Harry likes a drink. He usually drinks wine, but today he is drinking whisky. I am drinking whisky too, as I want to be like Harry.

'Have you noticed something different about me today, Scott?'

I look him up and down. The table is see-through, so I can see through it, can see his shoes through it, and his trousers, which are see-through.

'Something about my dress.'

I shake my head.

'It is unusually subdued,' Harry explains.

I nod. It is unusually subdued. His trousers may be see-through, but they are black. His shirt and shoes are black, and his tie is black.

'Oftentimes, my dress is garish, bordering on the attention-seeking. Today, it is unusually subdued.'

'Yes, but why?'

'I am in mourning. My partner of ten years has left me.'

'Doctor Bang?'

Harry nods, says nothing.

I also say nothing, hold my whisky to my nose, inhale.

'Sometimes in life, Scott, you have to make sacrifices. I sacrificed my love, my one true love, for my other one true love, television.'

I sit back, and think back to what Jim said to me all those months ago, over a surreal cigar at Bang House. You need to come up with an idea, Jim told me. An idea so good that Harry Maker will tell Doctor Bang to cock off.

Harry did tell Doctor Bang to cock off, but he didn't mean cock off out of my life, he meant cock off out of my career, for the time being at least. I am sorry, darling Bang, he would have said, but I am pulling the show. Real-Life Wood 'Shifters' can shift over. There is a new show in town, a variety show, hosted by an old friend of yours, a ghost giraffe named Jim.

Jim is not a ghost giraffe, Doctor Bang would have replied. He is a nigger. We used to hang him up by his shoelaces. And pick his nose. With the open end of an umbrella.

Harry returns from the bar with another glass of whisky, a double. 'I lie awake at night,' he tells me, sitting down, 'and think about what I have done, what I have lost. And do you know what, Scott? I feel a tremendous sadness. Right here.' He puts down his whisky and puts his hand on his heart. 'A tremendous television-shaped sadness.'

I blow my fringe. You can do this easily by jutting out your lower lip. This is all my fault, I say to myself as my fringe settles. But then, it is Doctor Bang's fault for having such a stupid idea. And Harry's for going along with it. My only crime, if crime is what it is, is being brilliant. More brilliant than both Harry and Doctor Bang put together.

Harry returns from the bar with another glass of whisky, another double. 'The only thing that has kept me going through all of this is the new show. Do you know what I think, Scott?' He raises his eyebrows so that they form the shape of a spaceship. 'I think it could go supernova.'

The main studio at Science Fiction Studios is called Studio One, though it is more affectionately known as the main studio, small m, small s. Space Man In Space was filmed in the main studio, as was the first series of the now discontinued spin-off show Under Water Man Under Water. It was in the main studio that Space Man fought the Two-Headed Three-Legged Four-Handed Lizard Man, and won. And it is in the main studio that Jim will capture the hearts of millions.

Harry and I are in the main studio now, surveying the set for the All New Jim Giraffe Variety Show. The studio has been turned into an old-fashioned theatre with a difference, the difference being that old-fashioned theatres are old-fashioned, and this theatre is not. The stage is hoofproof, designed to withstand many hours of high-density trotting. The giraffe pattern curtains are fashioned out of real giraffe skin, or what looks like real giraffe skin, and rise extra high to allow for Jim's extra high height.

But there is a problem. The lighting technician has never lit a ghost before and is unsure of how to deal with transparency. Ghosts are see-through, therefore, a certain percentage of the spotlight will pass through. If we allow for this by using a brighter spotlight, the lighting technician explains, some of the light will be absorbed by Jim's tuxedo and bounced back at the camera, causing a tuxedo-shaped glare. One way round it would be to apply the tuxedo afterwards using computer graphics, but the show is going out live, and anyhow Jim would have to perform in the nude.

It is a tense moment. The only sound is the tapping of fingers, the occasional clearing of a throat. All eyes turn to Harry Maker, as they are wont to do in times of crisis.

'Hmm,' I say, looking at Harry's trousers.

Harry looks down at his trousers. 'Why are you looking at my trousers?'

The lighting technician looks at Harry's trousers, too.

'Your trousers are see-through,' I explain. 'What if Jim were to wear a see-through tuxedo? It wouldn't absorb the light, and it wouldn't bounce it back at the camera.'

'Dear heart, I do believe you have got it.'

'He has got it,' the lighting technician confirms. 'In theory, at least. The question is, will it work in practice?'

There is only one way to find out. Harry has his assistant call the costume designer, Sassy Spark, and request that she meet us in make-up without delay.

Jim is pulling a face.

'There is nothing girly about make-up,' the make-up girl is saying.

'Then why do girls wear it?'

'To make them look pretty,' the make-up girl says, somewhat illogically. 'Hello, Scott,' she says, recognising my floppy blond fringe.

It takes me a moment to place her. 'Are you one of the make-up girls who does make-up for Space Man In Space?'

She doesn't say anything for a moment, she's trying to hold Jim's head still so that she can apply foundation to those funny little horn things. 'Yes,' she says. 'I do the make-up for Space Man.'

Jim's ears prick up. 'Does Space Man wear make-up?'

'Of course,' the make-up girl says. 'And he doesn't make a fuss neither.'

Jim nods. His neck muscles relax. He looks at his funny little horn things in the mirror, grins.

Sassy Spark comes into the room, surrounded by her entourage.

Harry shakes her by the fingertips. 'Sassy, how quickly can you knock up a see-through tux?'

'Lighting,' the lighting technician explains.

'For whom?'

'Jim,' Harry says.

Jim wrinkles his snout.

'But we have already performed for him a tuxedo,' Sassy says. 'Of the very finest quality.'

'Did you keep the pattern?'

'Sassy Spark does not use a pattern,' Sassy says. 'All Sassy Spark creations are performed ad hoc.'

'Well, that one is no good,' Harry says, pointing to a clothing rail, on which Jim's tuxedo is draped through half a dozen jangling coat hangers.

Sassy Spark is the highest paid costume designer in

television. Criticise one of her, um, creations and she is liable to go into a dead faint. Harry is on dangerous ground and he knows it. But then, Jim is set to become the biggest television star in television history, and Harry knows that too. After a brief conversation with her personal adviser, her therapist, her twelve-year-old boyfriend and her ninety-nine-year-old mother, Sassy agrees. 'But I will need cocaine,' Sassy says. 'And a new nose.'

The famous stand-up comic Bob Funny is practising his routine. You know Bob Funny. You have seen him on television, may even have seen him in concert, but you have to see him close up, backstage at Science Fiction Studios, to appreciate just how funny he really is.

His routine largely consists of a series of hilarious observations, cut through with an element of the surreal. 'Have you ever noticed,' Bob Funny asks his imagined audience, 'how on a double-decker bus it says no standing up upstairs? But you can't stand up upstairs. You fall over.' He pauses for comic timing, then says: 'Buses though. You wait ages for them, then three come along at once.'

Hmm. Anyhow, Jim is doing a final run-through with a troupe of dancing girls, the Legs Eleven. I have met this troupe before. Their leotards are so garish, whenever you meet them, you find yourself picking fragments of broken glass out of your eyeballs for a week.

'From the top,' Jim yells before launching into an elaborate tap routine. He doesn't need tap shoes. He has nature's tap shoes, otherwise known as hoofs.

'I learnt to tap in the jungle,' Jim told me in an exclusive interview earlier this week. 'Did I tell you about the fight I had with an elephant? He was firing peanuts at me through his trunk. Fortunately, I was brought up in the toughest part of the jungle, the east side, and at the first sign of trouble my legs are trained to trot on the spot.'

'But Jim,' I said, speaking directly into the tape recorder, 'I thought you said you were from Surrey.'

He chewed his lip.

'I suppose Surrey is in the jungle, is it?'

'Our garden was terribly overgrown.'

'Even so.'

He scratched his neck. 'We used to get a lot of wasps,' he said. 'I used to have to wear lotion.'

Wherever Jim learnt to tap, nobody can deny that he is good at it. His legs are a highly coordinated blur. Legs Eleven can barely keep up.

'Scott,' the head of the troupe says afterwards, 'I assume we are booked for the new series of Space Man In Space?'

I should point out at this point that one of Space Man's enemies is a race of aliens who communicate only through movement. 'Yes,' I confirm. 'We begin filming in the spring.'

'I hear you are having a baby,' one of the other dancing girls says.

'My wife is. My role is the role of provider.'

'Congratulations. When is the baby due?'

I look at my high-tech watch.

'Tonight?' the dancing girl says incredulous. 'Then why aren't you with your wife?'

I shrug. 'I want to watch the show.'

'But Scott, childbirth is the greatest show on earth.'

'We are having it filmed,' I explain defensively. 'I can watch it later, on video.'

'You can watch the All New Jim Giraffe Variety Show on

video. This is the birth of your first child, Scott. If you miss this, you will never—'

This last sentence is drowned out by an announcement over the loudspeaker. 'Thirty seconds till curtain.'

It may be drowned out by the loudspeaker, but it still resonates. 'Harry,' I say to Harry, 'I have to make a telephone call.' And I dash off. To make a telephone call.

The last time I spoke to Continence, the baby was starting to come out. It is likely, then, that the baby is now out, that I have missed it coming out. I press a button on my mobile phone and hold my mobile phone to my ear. 'Continence, has it come out?'

'Has what come out?'

'The baby. Has the baby come out?'

'No, Scott. There has been a complication. The baby started to come out, then went back in again.'

I take a deep breath. 'Continence, I'm coming home. Don't let it start to come out again until I get there. If it does start to come out, don't let it come all the way out,' I instruct. 'I want to be there for the birth.'

'But why?'

'I want to hold your hand. And watch the baby come out. I want to cut the cord. With a pair of purpose-bought scissors.'

She smiles. I hear the smile in her voice. 'Scott, I do love you.'

'I love you too, Continence.'

'But Scott, Doctor Apple is here, and he says that the baby won't come out until midnight.'

'Midnight?'

She nods. I hear the nod in her voice.

I perform some quick maths. 'The show finishes at half past ten. That gives me just enough time to watch the show, and attend the after-show party.'

Jim is a natural. The audiences give him a standing ovation. I only wish that my wife could be among them, or in the wings with Harry Maker and myself.

Or here, at the after-show party. Everyone else is here, including Single Mum Tum and her baby, Baby Bathwater. 'Congratulations,' Tum says, shaking me by the hand.

I wipe the sick on to my trousers and thank her.

'Me and Baby Bathwater enjoyed every minute of it, didn't we, Baby Bathwater.'

Baby Bathwater sicks up some more sick.

I pat Baby Bathwater on the head. 'Hello, Baby Bathwater.'

'It liked the animal thing, the giraffe thing. It likes animals, don't you, Baby Bathwater.'

Baby Bathwater nods, and sicks up some more sick.

'I have to get it home now, Scott. It's past its bedtime. That's why it keeps sicking things up. It always sicks things up when it's past its bedtime.'

Talking of sick, here comes one of my old school friends, Tinpot Wheeler. As you may recall, Tinpot Wheeler is the only boy ever to show me his willy. I had always doubted that Tinpot Wheeler would get on in life, so am not in the least surprised to find that he is still thirteen years old, is even wearing his old school uniform. He puts his hand into his blazer pocket, pulls out a crisp and stuffs it into his mouth. 'Want one?'

'No thank you.'

'Prawn cocktail. Nicked them from my dad's pub.' He

punches me between the legs, just like old times, and says: 'Do you know what spunk is?'

'Of course I know what spunk is. I'm a married man,' I boast. 'I am almost a parent.'

'Must be a flid then.' He picks his nose, his finger reaching deep into his brain. 'You going to that party? Lisa is having a party, at her house.'

I laugh. 'Why would I want to go to a party at her house, when I am welcome at high-profile media functions such as this?'

'Don't be a wanker, you flid.' He punches me in the stomach and runs off— straight into a big cake-shaped woman, who slaps him round the head and gives him a big cake-shaped hug, almost in the same movement.

'Hello, Mr Spectrum. Congratulations on the new show. The staff and I enjoyed it enormously.'

'Thank you, Nurse Matron.' I scratch my spectacles, though only the left lens. 'Gosh, putting on a show is hard work,' I tell her. She doesn't take the bait, so I add: 'Perhaps you could, um, administer one of your hugs?'

'Of course.' Halfway through the hug, she says: 'Who is that, waving at us from the far end of the party?' She hugs me a bit more, then says: 'He just waved again, right up close to my face.'

'It could be Vic Twenty, my best friend.' Nurse Matron and I rotate the hug one hundred and eighty degrees, so that my best friend and I are stood face to face. 'Vic.'

'How are you, Scott? How have you been?'

'Great. Did you watch the show?'

He shakes his head. 'I missed it,' he confesses. 'I was engrossed in a really interesting bit of computer programming and completely lost track of time.'

'Thanks again for writing that computer game, Vic. Jim hasn't stopped talking about it.'

'Anything for a friend, Scott. Anything that involves computer programming, that is. Can I get you a drink?'

'No,' I say, still reeling from my half a sniff of champagne. 'I am already drunk.'

'Not as drunk as that man over there.'

The man to whom he refers is Jonathan Cape, the man I met at the hospital. When he arrived he was wearing a business suit, like a businessman. He went round telling everyone that he was a superhero, that he would change into his superhero costume the moment anything exciting happened. Something exciting must have happened, as he now looks utterly ridiculous in sky-blue tights and the tight blue sweatshirt emblazoned with the letter C.

'I wonder if he has captured any criminals. Talking of criminals, isn't that that old woman who was sentenced to life imprisonment for the theft of indoor footwear?'

I think that he is joking at first, but when I follow his pointing finger I see Granny Bagpuss walking towards us. Being old, it takes her ages to get here, but, being an escaped convict, she is worth the wait. 'Hello, Scott.'

'Have you escaped from prison?'

She nods. 'I wanted to watch the show. They don't have television in prison, you see. Eddy was going to come to prison to visit me, but he never did, because of the television. Oh look, here he comes now.'

'Eddy,' I say, looking up at the underside of his chin. 'Did you enjoy the show, Eddy?'

'It was shit. Should've stayed at home, watched it on the telly.'

'But this was better than television, Eddy. It was real life.'

He looks confused, so I add: 'Real life is better than television, Eddy.'

'The way I look at it, is this. Everything, right, is shit.'

'Everything?'

He nods.

'What about Mr Bingo's suit? Is that shit?'

Eddy pulls a face. He doesn't know what I'm talking about.

'You know who Mr Bingo is,' I say, nodding towards the suburban pimp.

Eddy doesn't say anything, but I can tell from the expression on his face that he does.

'You said that everything is shit,' I tease. 'What about Mr Bingo's suit? Is that shit?'

Eddy looks at Mr Bingo, then at his business partner, Ape Hands, who does all the monkey work.

'No,' Eddy says. 'It's a nice suit. Not shit at all.'

Mr Bingo pats me on the back. 'I was just saying to Ape Hands here. Those dancing girls were the meat. Ain't that right, Ape Hands?'

Ape Hands nods.

'Jim told me how you rescued my girl from the seaside,' Mr Bingo says, straightening his tie. 'She ran away, Jim tells me, and you rescued her. Cigar, Ape Hands.'

Ape Hands takes a cigar from his suit pocket, lights it, and hands it to Mr Bingo.

'Another. For my friend here.'

Ape Hands lights another cigar, and hands it to me with his ape hands.

'If there is anything I can do, Scott, anything at all. I'm your biggest fan. Ain't that right, Ape Hands.'

Oh, I doubt that, I think to myself. My biggest fan is Spot Plectrum, founder of the Scott Spectrum Fan Club. As I mentioned earlier, Spot Plectrum isn't his real name. He changed it because he wanted to be like me. He even dresses like me. A natural redhead, he has his hair artificially straightened, bleached and fashioned into an unfashionable floppy fringe. Tonight he is dressed in top-of-the-range long-range spectacles, graph-paper trousers and non-slip anti-static socks, just like me. He is even wearing the same spaceship-shaped shoes.

When I say that he is my biggest fan, I should really say that he was my biggest fan but is my biggest fan no longer. All evening he has looked like he wanted to speak to me, but when he finally finds the courage he is too angry to formulate a sentence.

'I take it you didn't like the show.'

'You've sold out.' He takes off his top-of-the-range long-range spectacles and throws them on the floor. 'The Science Fiction Channel is a science-fiction channel,' he huffs and puffs. 'That,' he says, pointing vaguely in the direction of the main studio several floors up, 'was not science fiction.'

'How do you mean?'

'Science fiction is fiction. With a scientific bent,' he says, stamping on his top-of-the-range long-range spectacles. They don't break, so he stamps on them again. They don't break. 'That,' he storms, 'was not science fiction. It was light entertainment. With the emphasis on light.'

'It was definitely science fiction. I think.'

'Then where was the science?'

I chew my lip. 'The ghost.'

'Horror,' Spot says dismissively.

'The dancing girls.'

'Pornography.'

'Bob Funny.'

'Comedy.'

I chew my lip again. 'I have mouths to feed. One hour from now,' I say, looking at my high-tech watch and performing some quick maths, 'I will be a parent.'

'You've sold out. The Scott Spectrum Fan Club is disbanded. I will have my head shaved. And change my name back to Simon Horse.'

I stifle a laugh. 'Horse? Your surname is Horse?'

'So?'

'You should meet Jim. Simon Horse and Jim Giraffe.'

'I don't get it.'

'Animal surnames,' I say, laughing out loud. 'Jim will love this. Come on, come and meet Jim.'

He follows me somewhat reluctantly to the bar, where Jim has spent the entire party— I've just realised this— he's spent the entire duration of the party talking to the same man. I had always suspected that Jim was gay, and here is the proof. I find Harry, at the other end of the bar, and tap him on the shoulder. 'Jim is gay, Harry.'

Harry doesn't say anything to this, doesn't even look up.

'Sorry, that was rude of me. Harry, are you all right?'

'Do you know who that is?'

'No, who?'

'Max Gold, from the Platinum Channel.'

I look along the bar at Jim's companion.

'He approached Jim the moment he arrived, Scott. They've been talking ever since.'

I seat myself on a vacant bar stool. 'Harry, Jim is with us. He signed a ten-year contract. I witnessed it myself.'

'Look at Jim's front knees.'

I do so. 'He's resting them on the bar.'

'Look again.'

'All right, he's got them in the bar. He's a ghost, Harry. He can pass through things.'

'And you think a ghost is going to care about a poxy contract?'

I shrug.

'The Science Fiction Channel is over, Scott. Without Jim Giraffe, there is no All New Jim Giraffe Variety Show. And with no All New Jim Giraffe Variety Show,' Harry says, 'there is no money. That stage up there, that hoofproof stage. Have you any idea how much it cost? The entire budget for one series of Space Man In Space. Not one episode, Scott. One series.'

'Harry, the Science Fiction Channel is an institution. Part of the televisual landscape.'

Harry shakes his head. 'The Science Fiction Channel is a business. Well, it was a business.'

'But Harry, I have a wife, a child.'

'You're lucky. I,' Harry says, standing up, 'I have nothing.'

Harry is right. I am lucky. I have a wife, a child. Not that it has come out yet. Well, I hope it hasn't come out yet.

I had intended to get a taxi home and claim it on expenses, but Harry has frozen my expense account, so I have to get a train and make my own way from the station. When I reach the end of our road, I press a button on my mobile phone and hold my mobile phone to my ear. 'Continence, has it come out yet?'

'No, Scott, but it is coming out. You better get here soon, or you'll miss it.'

'I will. I got the train,' I inform her, 'and it broke down, so we had to get out and push.'

'You should have got a taxi.'

I don't say anything, just listen to my wife's breath, and my breath.

'You should have got a taxi, Scott. Why didn't you get a taxi?'

'There aren't any taxis,' I say, and in a sense there aren't. 'Continence, would you still love me if I didn't have any money?'

'Of course I would still love you. Why, are you thinking of leaving the Science Fiction Channel? Doctor Apple and I watched the show, didn't we, Doctor Apple.'

'Yes,' I hear Doctor Apple say. 'It was terrific. Hold on,' he says suddenly, 'the baby is starting to come out.'

'Don't let it come out. All the way out,' I say, fumbling with my front-door key. It won't go in, it won't turn— but it goes in, it turns— the door opens, I go in.

As I slam the front door, the lounge door opens and Doctor Apple comes out, wiping red stuff on his white medical coat. 'Congratulations. Your wife has just given birth to a bouncing baby giraffe.'

'A giraffe?'

Doctor Apple nods, smiles. 'A boy. Ten pounds, eleven ounces.'

'A giraffe?'

'A giraffe, yes.'

The room turns into a ship. I stagger to the side and vomit over the side.

A giraffe, a bouncing baby giraffe.

I wipe my chin on a tea towel, swallow something, go into the lounge.

Continence is sat in the high-tech birthing bed, her legs closed, a blanket over her legs. She looks at me, smiles. She looks down at the thing in her arms, smiles.

I step closer. I look at it, at Continence.

Doctor Apple puts on his coat, picks up his medical brief-case. 'What are you going to call it?'

I look at Continence. What are we going to call it?

'Jimmy,' Continence says. 'I want to call it Jimmy.'

Puppy Popper

As a member of the lazy army, the unemployed, I have been unable to provide for my wife and child. This makes me unhappy. It makes Continence unhappy, too. It causes arguments, usually involving chocolate. 'Did you buy me a bar of chocolate?' Continence will enquire on my return from the newsagent's.

'No,' I will reply. 'Just the newspaper.'

'I asked you to buy me a bar of chocolate,' Continence will say, putting little Jimmy into his high-tech highly portable cot, or taking him out of his high-tech highly portable cot. On this occasion, she is taking him out of it, to cuddle him.

'I couldn't afford it.' I perch on the edge of the high-tech birthing bed, open the newspaper and flick through to the job section. 'It was either the newspaper or the chocolate, and I opted for the newspaper. When I find a job, I will buy you a hundred chocolate bars. Or one big chocolate bar,' I tell her, 'the size of one hundred small chocolate bars.'

Continence picks up little Jimmy and cuddles him. 'Are there any jobs in there this week?'

'No.' I hold up the blank newspaper page. 'I am worried that I may never find a job. Science fiction is the only thing that I can do, Continence.'

'Hold Jimmy. It will take your mind off it.'

'I can't, I have to find a job.'

'Hold Jimmy,' Continence says, placing him in my reluctant arms.

I look down at little Jimmy, then look away. How Continence can deny that he is disabled, I do not know. His neck is abnormally long, as though Doctor Apple pulled him out by the head. His skin is covered in orange blotches. He has a club foot. Well, he has four club feet, and no hands. His nose is big. The top of his head is horribly disfigured, formed into two funny little horn things. His tongue is longer than a clown-shoe tongue. He can clean his ears with it. His ears are pointy, with tufts of orange hair. 'I wonder if there is anything on,' I say, referring to the television. 'There might be a repeat of Space Man In Space on the Repeat Channel.'

'Would you receive a fee?'

I shake my head. 'All repeat fees go to the Harry Maker Memorial Fund.'

'Poor Harry. He did take it bad.'

Yes, I think to myself. Poor Harry. As I think this, I inadvertently hold little Jimmy close to my chest, and he starts to cry. 'He's crying,' I say, stating the obvious.

'Then cuddle him.'

'I did cuddle him. That's why he's crying.'

'Hum to him,' Continence says. 'I have to get the front door.'

'Hum,' I hum. 'Hum hum hum hum hum.'

When Continence gets back, little Jimmy is still crying. 'Hum,' I hum. 'Oh, hello, Jim.'

'Hello, Scott,' Jim says.

'Sit down, Jim,' Continence says.

'I hope you wiped your hoofs, Jim.'

Jim looks down at his snow-covered hoofs. 'Sorry,' he says. 'I forgot.'

'You've left a trail of snow all the way from the front door.'

'Sorry.'

'Scott, don't be rude. Sit down, Jim,' Continence says. 'Scott will sweep that up, won't you, Scott.'

'If little Jimmy will stop crying. Jim, you hold him.' I put little Jimmy into Jim's arms, or front legs, and fetch a dustpan and brush from the kitchen. When I get back, I crouch on the carpet and sweep up the trail of snow. Snow is easy to sweep up when it is still snow. Leave it for a while and it will melt, and become water.

Continence looks at Jim, smiles. 'You do have a way with children, Jim.'

Jim says nothing, smiles. He's sat at one end of the sofa, holding little Jimmy. Continence is sat at the other end of the sofa. I dry the dustpan and brush on a tea towel, return the dustpan and brush to the cupboard and sit on the sofa, between Continence and the ghost giraffe.

'Jim is wonderful with little Jimmy,' Continence tells me. 'The moment he was in Jim's arms, or front legs, he stopped crying and smiled a big little Jimmy smile.'

I give Jim a look. He stands up, passes little Jimmy back

to Continence and sits back down. 'Have you found a job yet?'

'Not exactly. But I do have some interviews lined up.'

Continence sits forward, reaches round behind her back for the round brown cushion, her mum cushion, adjusts it and puts it back behind her back. 'Oh yes?'

'Yes,' I say, thinking fast. 'One is for a job as a pilot. One is for a job as a policeman. And one is for a job as a, um. Politician.'

Continence gives me a queer look. 'Funny how all of those jobs begin with the letter p, Scott.'

'Yes. Funny how the mind works.'

'I can get you a job,' Jim says.

'In television?'

'Films.'

'Films,' I repeat, taking it all in. 'I've always wanted to work in films. Um. Jim, what are you eating?'

'A chocolate bar.'

Continence sits forward again, looks round at me, at Jim. 'Chocolate?'

'I love chocolate bars,' Jim says, almost to himself. 'I have one hundred of them in the car.'

Continence licks her lips. 'You were going to buy me one hundred chocolate bars, weren't you, Scott. When you find a job.'

'Yes. Or one big chocolate bar,' I laugh. 'The size of one hundred small chocolate bars.'

No one says anything for a minute. Then, a minute later, Continence says: 'I wish I had one hundred chocolate bars.'

'You can have mine,' Jim says. 'If you like.'

Continence sits forward again. 'Can I?'

Jim shrugs.

Continence puts little Jimmy into his high-tech highly portable cot and follows Jim out to the car. After a few seconds of relaxing on the sofa with my newspaper, I step into my alien-shaped slippers, put on my snowproof thermal coat and run out through the front door.

Jim unlocks the boot of his electric-blue convertible sports car with an electric-blue electronic key, opens the boot, and there, in the boot, are one hundred chocolate bars, neatly stacked in piles of ten.

Continence looks at the chocolate bars, licks her lips.

'Go on,' Jim says, scooping up a hoof full, or hoofful, or hooful.

Continence scoops up a handful and stuffs them into one of the baggy pockets of her baggy brown mum trousers. She scoops up another handful and stuffs them into the other baggy pocket of her baggy brown mum trousers.

Jim looks at her, smiles.

Throwing all caution to the wind, Continence forms her brown breastfeeding sweatshirt into a holdall shape and fills it to the seams with chocolate bars, until the boot contains nothing but still-falling snow.

'Fill your boots,' Jim says. 'Fill your boots.' Continence is wearing sandals, not boots. I am wearing my alien-shaped slippers, and Jim has nature's boots, otherwise known as hoofs. So I take fill your boots to be an expression. As the ghost giraffe shuts the boot, Continence notices something on the back seat. The roof is down, the car is full of snow and the thing on the back seat is covered in snow.

'What's that?' Continence enquires. 'On the back seat.'

'Where?'

'Under the snow.'

'Oh,' Jim says. 'I thought you meant the snow.' He wipes

off some of the snow. 'It's a chocolate bar. A big one, the size of one hundred small chocolate bars.'

'May I have it?'

Jim looks at the chocolate bar, at my wife, shrugs. 'If you like.'

When Treetops Breath said that he could get me a job in films, he might more accurately have said that he could get me a job near films, as a cleaner in the local cinema.

I work with a working-class Scottish woman named Maggie Maggee, and like all working-class Scottish women, Maggie Maggee speaks in authentic Scottish vernacular. 'Ye pit the end oan here, like thon,' she tells me, picking up one end of the vacuum-cleaner pipe and pushing it into the vacuum cleaner. 'Then ye plug this in here, like, like this,' she says, plugging the power lead into a socket behind the foyer counter. 'Then, ye pit this in here, like this, and turn it oan, and ye clean it, like this.' She turns on the vacuum cleaner and proceeds to suck stray bits of popcorn from the inside of the glass-fronted popcorn dispenser.

'It doesn't look very hygienic.'

She shrugs. 'Ye'll git the hing ay it.'

With the cinema foyer clean, it is time for a tea break, before beginning the more daunting task of cleaning the cinema proper. Maggie Maggee takes a chocolate biscuit from her apron and places it on the table in front of me.

I look at the chocolate biscuit, at Maggie Maggee's hands. 'Your hands are dirty.'

'Ah've been workin here fir thirty year,' Maggie Maggee says, holding up her dirty hands. 'Muh ma worked here, and before that, her ma worked here. That wis back in the days when it wis a theatre.'

'Do you like working here?'

Maggie Maggee shakes her head.

'Then why do it?'

'It's whit ah dae,' she explains opaquely. 'Muh ma worked here, and her ma worked here, back in the days whin it wis a theatre.'

I stir my tea.

'Ma laddie worked here fir a while, at the tills. Eh goat caught wi ehs hand in the till, and goat the sack. It wasnae his fault though,' Maggie Maggee says in her son's defence. 'Eh goat mixed up wi drugs, and needed the money tae buy drugs.'

'Oh dear,' I say, stirring my dirty tea.

After work, Jim picks me up in his car. I have never been in his car before, or any other electric-blue convertible sports car with electric doors and electronic dashboard. It's snowing heavily, but we have the roof down to accommodate Jim's big ego, so the snow is landing on our heads. 'How can you afford this, Jim?'

'Do you like it?'

'It's a bit flash. I would have gone for something in grey. A grey space cruiser. With grey go-faster stripes.'

Jim laughs, shakes his head.

I straighten my spectacles. Everything still looks the same, so I unstraighten them again. 'Jim, you didn't answer my question.'

'What question?'

'I asked you how you can afford to own an electric-blue convertible sports car.'

'The new show.'

'The new show?'

'For the Platinum Channel, Spec. It starts this Saturday. The Jim Giraffe Dancing Girls Experience.'

I wriggle my nose. A snowflake lands on it, so I wriggle it again, and the snowflake falls off. 'Why is it called The Jim Giraffe Dancing Girls Experience?'

'It's an experience,' Jim says opaquely. 'With dancing girls in it.'

'But in what sense is it an experience?'

Jim looks nonplussed, so I elaborate.

'Are the dancing girls part of the experience? Or are they the experience?' I suggest. 'In which case, who experiences the experience? You, or the girls themselves? Or they, the viewers, watching at home?'

Jim shrugs. You can tell he is new to television.

'Well, I won't be watching it.'

'Suit yourself.'

'It's sexist, for one thing. Those girls are being exploited.'

'Not during the show. If I exploit them, it'll be after the show, in the dressing room.'

'Dancing girls aren't objects, Jim. They're human beings, like you and me. Well, like me. And should be appreciated for their minds. Your show is sordid,' I scold. 'And I will not under any circumstances be tuning in.'

'Your loss.'

'And why is it my loss?'

'There's free pizza for every viewer.'

'Free pizza?'

'Max Gold's idea. There'll be an advert half an hour before the show, inviting the viewer to order a pizza from their local pizza parlour. They pay for it in the usual way, then, towards the end of the show, a telephone number flashes on the screen, and they have to call it and claim back the cost of the pizza.'

'Why towards the end of the show?'

'To get them to watch the show.'

'Of course. But surely they miss the show, while they're making the call?'

'Who cares,' Jim says brazenly. 'The number flashes up just before Bob Funny.'

'You've got Bob on the show?'

Jim nods.

'It isn't just dancing girls then?'

'Dancing girls, me and Bob.'

'So why isn't it called The Jim Giraffe Dancing Girls And Bob Funny Experience?'

Jim wipes the snow from the funny little horn things on the top of his head with his right front hoof. 'I think it was because we want it to have a good name, and The Jim Giraffe Dancing Girls Experience is a good name. Anyway, it might not always be Bob Funny. We might get someone else on. The Hilarity Twins. Or that surrealist ventriloquist, Samuel Surreal And His Surreal Seal, Saul.'

'Samuel who?'

'Surreal.'

'And his—'

'Surreal Seal, Saul.'

'Saul?'

Jim nods.

'Samuel Surreal And His Surreal Seal, Saul?'

'That's what I said, Spec. Samuel Surreal And His Surreal Seal, Saul.'

I remove my spectacles, wrinkle my forehead and replace my spectacles. 'Is Samuel the name of the ventriloquist? And he's surreal, so his name is Surreal. Like Bob Funny is funny, so his surname is Funny. Yes, and the Hilarity

Twins are hilarious, if you like that sort of thing.'

Jim isn't listening. He reaches over to my side of the car, opens the glove compartment and takes out two glasses, one each, I presume, one for me and one for him. He reaches beneath his seat, produces a bottle of champagne, uncorks the cork with his corkscrew tail, fills the two glasses, drinks the champagne from one, throws it into the snow, drinks the champagne from the other one and throws it into the snow.

'And the seal is surreal too,' I say, pretending not to notice, 'so his surname is Surreal, too. Samuel Surreal And Seal Surreal.'

Jim shakes his head. 'You got it wrong.' He leans over the side of the car and pours the remaining champagne into the snow. 'Don't drink the yellow snow,' he says ominously. 'The seal is just called Saul.'

'But you just told me that his surname is Surreal.'

'You're thinking of Samuel,' Jim says. 'Samuel is surreal, so his surname is Surreal.'

'Is the seal surreal?'

'Yes.'

'But his surname isn't Surreal?'

'No, he's just called Saul.'

'Saul Seal.'

'Not even that. Just Saul,' Jim says. 'He couldn't be called Saul Seal, it would be too confusing.'

'How so?'

'The act would be called Samuel Surreal And His Surreal Seal, Saul Seal.'

'Animal surnames,' I muse, scratching my spectacles. 'This friend of mine, Spot Plectrum, he has an animal surname.'

'A plectrum isn't an animal.'

'Plectrum isn't his real name,' I explain. 'His real name is Simon Horse.'

'Horse?'

I nod.

'Is he a horse?'

'No. He's human.'

'Then why isn't he called Simon Human?'

'Never mind all that,' I say, tapping the electric-blue electronic dashboard. 'Take me for a spin.'

Jim doesn't need telling twice. He turns the key, puts his hoof to the floor and we're away.

'Wow! It's fast.'

He nods.

A few minutes later, as we emerge from the far end of the suburbs, I say: 'You do drive fast, Jim.'

He nods. He's got his head back. The wind plays tunes on his bared teeth.

'When I say you drive fast,' I clarify, 'I mean that you drive too fast, that you should slow down.'

He nods, says nothing.

'Jim, can you slow down a bit, please?'

He does. But only because we crash into a lamp post.

'Ha ha ha,' Jim laughs maniacally. 'Ha ha ha ha ha.'

'That will teach you to show off,' I say, as my airbag deflates.

'It won't. I've done it every day for the past week, and I haven't learnt a thing.'

'How can you have done it every day? Don't tell me, this is a ghost car. You can crash it to your heart's content, and no damage is done.'

'There's no such thing as a ghost car,' Jim says, quite reasonably.

'You have a fleet of mechanics, then, who can have it

fixed up in no time, have it ready first thing in the morning.'

'Nothing that extravagant. I simply use one of my other cars.'

'How many cars have you got?'

'One hundred.'

'One hundred electric-blue convertible sports cars, all the same?'

He nods.

'And you crash them all, one a day, into an item of street furniture, at the taxpayer's expense?'

He nods, grins.

'You're a menace,' I say, as smoke rises from the crumpled bonnet. 'And you should be locked up.'

'I'd like to see them try. If they couldn't keep an old granny behind bars, how can they expect to lock up a ghost?'

'We could be about to find out.'

'How so?'

I point my arched eyebrows at the rear-view mirror. A uniformed man is approaching, a policeman. He looks like one of the policemen from that television programme, Cops R Tops. We watch him in the mirror, then we look up and he's stood beside us, he's real.

The policeman looks at the car, at the wheels. Scratches his famous face. Looks at me, the unemployed scriptwriter, at Treetops Breath, the starry-eyed ghost giraffe, his hoofs gripping the wheel. 'Is this your vehicle?'

Jim doesn't say anything.

'Aren't you one of the cops from Cops R Tops?' I enquire.

'Yes, that's right.'

'Inspector Blue?'

'Inspector Black,' the policeman says. 'Inspector Blue is the one with the bad temper.'

'It's all right,' I tell Jim in an aside, 'he isn't a real policeman, he's an actor.'

Jim pokes out his tongue, laughs. 'I drank a bottle of champagne, and crashed my car.'

'And I robbed a bank,' I joke. 'I took all of the money, and ran away.'

'I robbed a river bank,' Jim says. 'Ate all the fish.'

'Yes,' I say, getting carried away, 'and we came back and ate all the water, and the river bank, and the sky.'

Inspector Black takes out his notebook, writes something down. 'Jim Giraffe, I am placing you under arrest. For crashing a moving vehicle. While under the influence of alcohol.'

'What about me? I stole the sky.'

'Don't push it,' Inspector Black says. 'I may be an actor, but that doesn't mean that I'm not a real policeman too.'

I swallow. 'Are you a real policeman?'

Inspector Black takes out his police badge, shows it to me, to Jim. 'As a matter of fact, I am.'

'Oh.'

Inspector Black is just about to fasten his handcuffs or hoofcuffs around Jim's front hoofs, his driving and nose-picking hoofs, when Jim blurts out: 'Couldn't we talk about this? I work in television, I can make you a star.'

'I'm already a star. I'm on Cops R Tops.'

'Your own show,' Jim says. 'Platinum Channel, Saturday nights. You put those cuffs away, I'll have a word with Max Gold.'

Inspector Black folds up the handcuffs, or hoofcuffs, hangs them over his belt, and walks off, muttering something about dancing girls.

'I must say, Jim, you handled that very well. Kept your cool. Which is more than I can say for me. But then, you have your own show, don't you. And I don't. I don't have anything. And that isn't cool at all.'

Jim nods. Reaches over to my side of the car. Opens the glove compartment. Pulls out his sunglasses. Puts them on. Grins.

'Jim, it's snowing, it's the middle of winter. You look like an idiot.'

But he doesn't look like an idiot. He looks cool.

I'm looking at Jim's reflection in the rear-view mirror, thinking about how cool he looks, when his image is blocked by another image, that of a uniformed man, a policeman. I think it is Inspector Black at first, coming back. But it isn't. It's Inspector Blue, the one with the bad temper.

'Hello, officer. Jim, look who it is.'

Inspector Blue looks at the car, at the wheels. At the smug yellow git behind the wheel, his hoofs up on the dashboard, his eyes hidden behind sunglasses, designer sunglasses, designed by Denim England, the coolest fashion designer in England.

'Jim, tell Inspector Blue about the bottle of champagne you drank, just before you crashed your car.'

'He doesn't have to,' Inspector Blue says. 'I can smell it on his breath.'

Jim sits up, puts his face close to Inspector Blue's face, blows a gust of ghastly ghost breath into Inspector Blue's face.

Inspector Blue steps back, pulls out his notebook, writes something down. 'Jim Giraffe,' he says, brushing snow from the top of his helmet, 'I am placing you under arrest.'

Continence is trying to put little Jimmy into his high-tech highly portable cot, but he won't fit. He has always had a long neck, and it seems to be getting longer.

'Children grow so fast,' Continence says, carefully avoiding any mention of Jimmy's deformity.

I tighten my job-interview tie. 'We'll have to buy him a new cot.'

'We can't afford a new cot,' Continence says, lifting little Jimmy clear of the high-tech highly portable cot and laying him along the sofa. 'Not a high-tech highly portable one anyway.'

'If I get this job—'

'What is the job?'

'Um. Porter. At a hotel.'

'I have to go into town, Scott. I can give you a lift.'

'But you haven't got a car.'

'I have Jim's car,' Continence says, jangling Jim's car keys. 'He asked me to look after it, while he's in prison.'

'You can drop me off just here, by the psychiatric institute.'

Continence gives me a funny look, though only briefly, as she is driving. Cars are dangerous, particularly electric-blue convertible sports cars. 'Why do you want to get out here? I thought the interview was at a hotel.'

'The job is at a hotel, but the interview is here, at the psychiatric institute.'

Continence parks the car at the side of the road, outside the psychiatric institute, applies the handbrake, and gives me another funny look.

I get out of the car, slam the car door, and watch my wife drive away. It is snowing heavily, so much so that the car roof is already covered in snow. As she drives away, the snow falls off.

The receptionist invites me to take a seat, but just as I am about to take it, a door opens and a black-bearded man invites me into his office. The nameplate on the door reads: Dr Z Fraud, Mental Psychiatrist.

'Now,' Doctor Fraud says as I hang up my coat, 'what seems to be the problem?'

'It's my brain, Doctor,' I confide. 'I think it's going.'

'Going?'

'Going,' I repeat. 'As in, going going gone.'

'And what makes you think that your brain is going?'

I recline on the leather couch, make myself comfortable. 'It all started when I began to receive visitations from a ghost giraffe. He would step out of the wardrobe—'

'Jim Giraffe?'

'That's right, yes. Have you heard of him?'

'Of course I've heard of him. He has his own show. The Platinum Channel, Saturday nights.'

'Thank goodness for that,' I say, sitting up. 'I thought I was going mad.'

'Where are you going?'

'Home,' I say, putting on my coat.

'Scott, the fact that a person does not hallucinate does not make him or her sane. If that were so, I would be out of a job. Now, lie on the couch and tell me about your childhood.'

'Well, it all began when I was born—'

'Was it a traumatic birth, Scott?'

'I don't remember.'

'Repression,' Doctor Fraud says, lighting a trumpet-shaped cigarette. 'Or is it regression?'

I shrug, always an odd thing to do while lying down.

Doctor Fraud pulls a book down from a shelf, thumbs through, mutters the word hmm, closes it and returns it to the shelf. 'Tell me something about your relationship with your own children, Scott. If you have children, that is.'

'I do have one child. Our relationship is not good,' I admit. 'He's disabled, you see, and I don't like that sort of thing.'

'Well, who does?' Doctor Fraud says, lying beside me on the couch.

'His neck is abnormally long,' I state factually, 'and the top of his head is horribly disfigured, formed into two funny little horn things—'

'Like those found at the top of a giraffe,' Doctor Fraud suggests.

'Yes. And he has a club foot. Well, he has four club feet—'

'Hoofs.'

'A bit like hoofs, yes. His ears are pointy, with tufts of orange hair, and his skin is covered in orange blotches—'

'Giraffe pattern,' Doctor Fraud says, standing up and pacing the room. 'It sounds to me, Scott, as though your wife has given birth not to a human child but to a giraffe.'

'It's funny you should say that, but Doctor Apple— the family doctor, who was present at the birth— said that it was a giraffe. I remember it as though it were yesterday. He was wiping red stuff on his coat, his white coat. Congratulations, he said. Your wife has given birth to a bouncing baby giraffe.'

Doctor Fraud nods, sucks smoke from his trumpet-shaped cigarette.

'I had forgotten about that.'

'It must have come as quite a shock.'

'I don't remember,' I say with a heavy sigh. 'The next few weeks were a blur. I can't remember anything until—'

'Until what?'

'I can't remember.'

'Well, what can you remember?'

'My wife took it worse than me. She wouldn't even admit that our child is disabled.'

'Well, maybe he isn't disabled, maybe Doctor Apple was right.'

'But my wife is a human being. How can she have given birth to a giraffe?'

'Could she have been impregnated by a giraffe?'

'She doesn't know any giraffes. Well, there's Jim, but Jim's my friend.'

'Is he?'

I don't answer that, too busy surveying the room. There are a lot of plants, and above Doctor Fraud's desk is a plaque reading: It is they who are mad.

'Where was the child conceived?'

'At the seaside. It was the first time my wife and I had sex. The only time we've had sex.'

'Did you enjoy it?'

'Yes,' I say, hiding behind my spectacles.

'What position did you do it in?'

'I was standing up. And my wife was sat in front of me, on the sand.'

'And then what happened?'

'We went back to the hotel, and had a bath.'

'You had intercourse in the bath?'

'No, we had separate baths.'

'And then what happened?'

'We went to see a film.'

'You had intercourse in the cinema?'

'No.'

'And then—'

'We went home, and went to bed.'

'You had intercourse in bed?'

'No, Doctor. We went to sleep.'

Doctor Fraud opens the window, throws the remainder of his trumpet-shaped cigarette out of the window, and closes the window. 'Scott, a woman cannot become pregnant through oral sex,' Doctor Fraud explains. 'It is physically impossible.'

I nod. 'Can I go now?'

'If you wish.'

I get up off the couch, put my coat on, and go.

Out in the snow, the snow is snowing more heavily than ever. As a countermeasure, I decide to call Continence and ask her to pick me up in Jim's car.

As I pull my mobile phone from my trouser pocket, it emits a loud ringing sound. Usually it is funny when it does that, but on this occasion it is not funny at all, as it makes me jump, and I drop it, and it falls down a drain. I crouch on my hands and knees and insert my hands into the drain. My hands freeze up and fall off, and I fall over.

Giving up, I stand up, brush the snow from my graph-paper trousers and begin the long walk home. I have barely gone two paces when my legs freeze up and fall off, and I fall over.

It is at that moment that a car pulls up beside me, not an electric-blue convertible sports car, sadly, but a taxi. I explain to the taxi driver that I do not have any money, that I am a member of the lazy army, the unemployed, and he drives off.

I am just about to give up, to collapse in the snow and die, when a hand taps me on the shoulder. I turn round, and another hand opens my hand and fits something into it, a bottle of something. Another hand, or possibly the first hand again, pushes the bottle to my lips. The bottle contains whisky.

The stranger introduces himself, but his name gets lost in the snow the moment it leaves his lips. 'It's tough out here,' he tells me, leading me to a campfire beneath the railway arches. 'We vagrants must stick together.'

'I'm not a vagrant. I'm a pedestrian. I've just come out of the psychiatric institute—'

'It started out that way with me,' the vagrant says. His face is hidden by snow, so I can't see his face, just the snow.

'What did?'

'The slide. From the top,' the vagrant says, raising his hand, 'to the bottom,' he says, lowering his hand. He lowers it very low, almost to the snow.

'I'm not on the slide. Quite the opposite, in fact. I'm on the ladder.'

'The ladder that leads up to the top of the slide,' the vagrant says, taking a swig of whisky.

I am about to object when I realise that I don't know what he is talking about, so instead I grab the bottle of whisky and take a swig.

No one says anything for a bit, so the strange man screws the cap back on to the bottle and says: 'I wasn't always a vagrant, you know. I was a happily married man. I had a job, a home.'

'Oh yes?'

'One day, my business partner, Tim, took a job at a rival company. Without Tim, our company went down the pan, and I went down with it.'

'Something similar has happened to me.'

'Just when I thought things couldn't get any worse, I caught my wife in bed with another man. That man, Scott,' the vagrant says, unscrewing the cap from the whisky bottle, 'was Tim. My business partner. My best friend.'

'My best friend would never do that to me. He's far too respectable. And besides,' I say in Jim's defence, 'he's in prison.'

The moment I say the word prison, I realise where I am. On the other side of the railway track is Suburbia Low Security Prison, a low-security prison situated by the railway track, in suburbia.

Why Jim hasn't escaped, I do not know. Perhaps he has decided to repay his debt to society, accept the punishment that the authorities have given him, turn over a new leaf. More likely he is just humouring them.

I shake the snow from my shoes and make my way across the lobby to the low-security security desk. 'I'm here to see a friend of mine,' I tell the security man. 'Jim Giraffe.'

After a series of low-security security checks, I am shown through a series of doors and into a large, brightly lit room, in which dozens of uniformed prisoners chat casually with their respective visitors. As I make my way across the room, my pace begins to slow. Jim sticks out like a sore thumb, a tall, yellow sore thumb, with a big nose. He already has a visitor, a woman, dressed all in brown. I can see Jim, but he can't see me, he doesn't know that I'm here. I know this because he has his tongue down the woman's throat.

Bring on
the dancing girls

Today, after serving just three months of his ten-year sentence, Treetops Breath is to be released from prison. Continence, little Jimmy and I are here to meet him. The lover, the illegitimate child and the former best friend.

Continence parks the electric-blue convertible sports car in the visitors' car park, close to where she parked it on that ill-fated winter afternoon, when I first caught the pair of them at it. It is spring now, one year since TB and I first met. And what a year it has been. A disjointed year, with bits stuck on it.

The prison doors open and TB comes out, a cardboard box strapped to his back. He would have it under one arm, but he's a giraffe.

Continence steps forward to meet him, then stops and looks at me, seeking approval. I nod reluctantly, and she runs across the car park and gives TB a big tonsil snog.

I wait here, by the car. Little Jimmy is asleep on the back seat. Continence has the roof down, to accommodate TB's long neck, his long, bogey-filled nose, and their love, which floats above them like a heart-shaped bogey-filled balloon.

'I want to drive,' TB says, reaching for the car door. He stops, smiles at her, adds: 'If I may.'

Continence nods. She sits beside him in the front, and I sit in the back with little Jimmy. Why we still refer to him as little I do not know, for he has grown almost as big as you or me.

'You've no idea how good it feels to be out here, breathing fresh air, that sort of caper.'

Continence nods her head. Her straight brown hair is tied back in a straight brown shape, tied with a round brown hair-tie. When she nods her head, the straight brown shape nods too.

'This car,' TB says, tapping the electronic dashboard, 'I have driven this car every night for the past three months. In my dreams, I mean,' he adds for the sake of clarity.

Continence puts her hand on his hoof, his gearstick hoof, and the hand remains there as he slips the car into gear and we pull away.

'I want to take you to my favourite restaurant. You too, Scott,' TB says, raising his eyebrows at me in the rear-view mirror.

'Will they have a highchair for little Jimmy?' Continence enquires, giving TB a look of very real concern.

TB shrugs. He doesn't know.

'We should have brought the high-tech birthing bed,' Continence says, taking TB's arm. 'Scott has had it converted into an outsized high-tech highchair.'

TB looks at me, smiles. 'Is that right?'

I nod.

The waiter leads us across the crowded restaurant, up a flight of stairs, up another flight of stairs, and up a silver-plated spiral stairwell to a revolving circular room on the roof. 'This,' the waiter explains, indicating a table in the centre of the room, the only table in the room, 'is our penthouse table. The penthouse table is reserved only for members of the royal family, recently returned explorers, and those who have their own television show.' He pulls out TB's chair, and TB sits. He pulls out a chair for Continence, and she sits too. The waiter doesn't pull out a chair for me. There are no chairs left. 'Forgive me. I will fetch another chair.'

I stand by the window, chew my thumbs. You can see all of suburbia from here. As the room revolves, you get to see the bits that you cannot see, the hidden bits. If you look closely, you can see my house. Our house. The house in which I live with my wife, and her bastard child.

'Little Jimmy will never fit in that,' Continence says. The waiter has returned with a highchair. 'It's too small.'

'It only looks small because it is far away,' the waiter explains. 'This room is deceptively shaped, like an optical illusion.' The waiter moves the chair forward, and, sure enough, it gets bigger.

Continence and I lift up little Jimmy and insert him into the chair.

'Waiter,' TB says, snapping his hoofs as you or I might snap your or my fingers, 'we will start with a starter. And a bottle of your finest champagne. I've just come out of prison, you know.'

'We know. And don't we know it.'

'Scott, don't be rude. Jim has just come out of prison.'

'And that is a good thing, is it?' She avoids my gaze, so I

elaborate. 'There is nothing good about coming out of prison, Continence. Coming out of prison means just one thing. That you have been in prison. And that means just one thing. That you are a criminal, that you have committed a crime.'

'Jim is a television star,' Continence says in TB's defence. 'All television stars go to prison these days, don't they, Jim? I read about it in a magazine.'

TB nods. 'Max Gold reckons it will double the viewing figures.'

'We think the show is wonderful, don't we, Scott?' Continence says, toying with her round brown hair-tie, as she is wont to do.

I shake my head. Though only in my head. The outside of my head doesn't move.

'Scott and I think it was very brave of you, Jim, to continue the show from prison.'

Brave. That's one word for it. Another word for it is stupid, or idiotic. One week, they dressed the troupe of dancing girls as a troupe of dancing inmates, covered in porridge.

The waiter comes back, carrying a huge bottle of champagne and three cut-glass crystal glasses. He places the glasses on the table, opens the bottle of champagne, spraying the revolving room with champagne-coloured foam, and fills each of the three cut-glass crystal glasses with champagne. He passes a glass each to Continence and TB. 'For the happy couple.'

'What about me? Do I get a glass of champagne, or is this one for little Jimmy?' I pick up the remaining glass, put it to my lips and inhale.

When I regain consciousness, Continence and TB have finished the starter and started on the main course. It is difficult to eat while standing up, particularly with everyone else sat down. The problems are social as well as practical. For example, I could ask TB to pass the duck ping pong, but if I am standing up I might just as well reach over and get it myself.

Continence gazes lovingly into TB's eyes, and asks him why he was released from prison nine years and nine months early.

'I have my own show,' TB explains, somewhat predictably. 'The prison governor is a big fan. He loves the dancing girls. And Bob, of course. Everyone loves Bob Funny.'

'Bob hasn't been on recently,' Continence observes.

TB shakes his head. 'Bob was sent to prison,' he explains, 'for abusing young boys.'

'But surely, if Bob is in prison—'

'Prisoners aren't allowed to appear on television, Continence. Unless they have their own show of course,' TB says. 'There are a lot of perks for those of us who have our own show.'

'Huh,' I huh, munching on a slice of duck ping pong. 'It sounds to me that you were living a life of luxury.'

'I had a cell all to myself. Shagpile carpet, en suite bathroom, the works.'

Continence smiles, says nothing.

'It wasn't all fun and games though. I met some very dodgy characters. Criminals, mainly. One bloke was in for armed robbery.'

I shake my head. 'Hang on, if this man was in for armed robbery, why was he in a low-security prison?'

'He was a colleague of a certain Mr Bingo,' TB explains.

'The suburban pimp?'

TB nods. 'They had him in a maximum-security prison, in the middle of the sea. Mr Bingo had a word with the judge, and they reduced his sentence from ten years to ten days, and transferred him to Suburbia Low. Nice bloke,' he adds. 'I used to beat him at cards.'

'I would have let him win.'

Continence gives me a look of contempt. 'You would.'

'What about you, Scott?' TB says, changing the subject. 'What have you been up to these past three months?'

I shrug.

'Are you still working at the cinema?'

I shake my head.

'Have you found a new job?'

'Yes,' I state optimistically. 'Well, no.'

TB nods. Picks up the remainder of the duck ping pong. Puts it into his mouth. Swallows. Wipes his chin. Holds back his head. Laughs.

The only thing that gets me through the meal is the thought of spending an evening at home with my wife. But Continence has invited TB round for evening drinks. Worse, he arrives with two friends, a rock-star ghost giraffe named David Giraffe, also known as Dave, and a celebrity-chef ghost giraffe named Andrew Giraffe, also known as Andy. Worse still, they bring their wives with them, two inter-changeable blonde women named Carla and Carol. Why ghost giraffes can't marry other ghost giraffes I do not know. They come over here, take our women, et cetera.

'This is Carol,' TB says, taking Carla's coat, 'and this,' he says, taking Carol's coat, 'is Carla.'

'Hello,' Continence says.

I don't say anything.

'Come through to the lounge,' Continence says. 'Scott, would you like to fetch the wine?'

I wouldn't, but I do, as I don't know what else to do. I take the bottle of wine from the fridge, pour it into six wine glasses, place the six wine glasses on a tray, and carry the tray through to the lounge.

Andy and Dave are sat on the couch with Carol and Carla, Continence is sat in TB's lap in one of the armchairs and little Jimmy is in his outsized high-tech highchair. I, of course, have to stand.

'What a lovely highchair,' Carla says. 'Where did you get it?'

'Scott had it converted from a high-tech birthing bed,' Continence explains, 'which he'd had converted from a high-tech armchair.'

'Oh,' Carla says, giving me a look of contempt.

'Is little Jimmy a ghost giraffe,' Carol asks, changing the subject, 'or a regular giraffe?'

'A regular giraffe,' Continence tells her.

'Your hair looks nice, Conti,' Carla says, referring to my wife's hair, which she has had bleached blonde to match Carla and Carol's.

'You should've dyed it black, like mine,' Dave says, referring to his hair, which is dyed black. Dave is the lead singer of a gothic rock band, the Dead Giraffes, and dresses accordingly. He has black hoof polish and black eyeliner, and wears a silver pendant around his neck, in the shape of a cross.

'Where did you two meet, Conti?' Carol enquires conversationally.

Continence sips her wine, sits forward in TB's lap, and says: 'Oh, we've known each other for years.'

'Years? But I've only known him for one year. And I met him first.'

Continence ignores me, continues to talk as though I am not here. 'I used to work in a sex shop. Jim would pop in every week, to buy pornography. He asked me to help him try on a leather playsuit. In the changing room, he reached over and kissed me, and we started seeing each other. This went on for eight years. Eight years. Then, one day, Jim said that he was tired of being the other giraffe— that's like being the other woman, but taller— and could we have a baby, settle down.'

TB rests his yellow-blue chin on the top of her head, on her bleached-blonde hair. 'She was worried about Scott, so I said I'd have a word with him, explain.'

'Well, you didn't do a very good job of it,' I say, but nobody seems to hear.

'And how did he take it?' Carol enquires.

Continence blushes.

TB squeezes her hand with his hoof, whispers something in her ear, something like: Go on.

'Actually, Jim and I have an announcement to make.' Continence takes a deep breath, removes her round brown hair-tie from her bleached-blonde hair, drops it into the waste-paper basket, and says: 'Jim and I are getting married.'

Carla and Carol stand up, hug her, kiss her. Andy and Dave slap TB on the back, shake his hoof.

'Scott,' TB says, 'get the champagne.' I don't do anything, I don't get the champagne, so he looks me square in the eye and says: 'Scott, champagne.'

I just stand here, shake my head. 'Continence, you can't.'

'Can't what?'

I don't say anything.

'What can't I do, Scott?'

'Get married. You can't get married, Continence. You're already married. To me.'

'We can get a divorce.'

TB holds out some papers. 'I have the papers right here.'

'If you think I'm signing those—'

'You have to.'

I don't. I can just stand here, do nothing.

I stand here for a number of minutes, doing nothing, with the three women and the three ghost giraffes sipping champagne and making jokes, some of which are about me.

Carla chinks Continence's glass. 'Where are you going to live, Conti?'

Continence kisses TB on the flank. 'Paradise. Jim is renting a villa, in paradise.'

I want to come too, I say childishly, though only in my head. I want to come to paradise with you. And watch you have fun. 'What about the house? Who gets the house?'

Continence looks at me and says: 'You get the house.'

'Of course I do. It's my house. Well, our house.'

'You get the house,' TB says, 'but you have to sign the papers. It's all here, in black and white.' And it is of course. It says: Clause 25b. Scott gets the house.

'All right. I'll sign.'

Continence, my wife, hands me a pen, and I sign the papers and return the pen to Continence, my ex-wife.

'It's a nice house,' Carol says.

'I like the suburbs,' Carla says. 'It's a shame they're going to be bulldozed.'

'Bulldozed?'

TB looks at me and says: 'Haven't you heard?'

'Heard what?'

'The suburbs are going to be bulldozed. I bought them,'

he explains. 'I'm building a car park, a park-and-ride.'

'You can't build a car park here,' I protest. 'I won't have anywhere to live.'

TB shrugs.

'Please,' I plead. 'Please don't bulldoze the suburbs. The suburbs are beautiful. Without the suburbs, I'm nothing.' He doesn't respond. 'Please, Jim. I'll do anything.'

TB gives the matter some thought, then says: 'Sign the house back over to me. I will live here, with my family. With Conti, and little Jimmy.' He holds out some more papers, and a pen.

I sign the papers and sigh a heavy, drawn-out sigh. 'So where am I supposed to live?'

TB shrugs, he doesn't care.

'Can I stay here, with you? I'll be very quiet. You won't even know I'm here.'

TB gives the matter some thought, then gives it some more thought, and says: 'Fine. But only for a few days, just until you get yourself sorted out. And you'll have to stay in the wardrobe. If I see your ugly mug, I'll hoof it.'

That ghost giraffe has taken everything. My wife, my home, my career. Even my floppy blond fringe has lost its veneer, and all because of him. TB. Treetops Breath. The ghost giraffe nigger. From the jungle.

I'm just thinking these thoughts, over and over and over, though not necessarily in that order, when the wardrobe door opens and I fall out.

Jim straightens his bow tie. 'I'm getting married today. Hooray!'

'How long have I been in there?'

'All day. Since yesterday.'

I look at my high-tech watch. 'Barry will be here in a minute, to collect my things.'

'Are you moving in with Barry?'

'Just for a few days,' I say defensively. 'While I get myself sorted out.'

'Where does Barry live? Doesn't he live downstairs, under the sink?'

'Haven't you heard? The council gave him a flat. In Hemel Hempstead.'

Jim nods, not really listening. There is a mirror on the inside of the wardrobe door, and he is using it to check his look.

I clap my hands. 'Right. I had better get my things.'

'What things?'

'My things.'

'You haven't got any things.'

'Haven't I?'

Jim shakes his head. 'Conti threw them all away.'

'What about my high-tech-armchair-cum-high-tech-birthing-bed-cum-outsized-high-tech highchair?'

'You can have that if you like,' Jim says, leading me down the stairs. 'Denim has designed us a new one, as a wedding present.'

'Denim?'

'Denim England, the coolest fashion designer in England.'

The doorbell rings. It's Barry, come to collect my things, or should I say thing. With the flick of a switch, I convert it back into a high-tech armchair. Jim helps me carry it out to the front garden and strap it on to Barry's back.

'Well, this is it, I guess,' Jim says.

I nod.

'Nice doing business with you, Spec.'

I nod, say nothing.

Jim holds out his hoof for me to shake, but I don't shake it.

'Don't worry about Conti.' He holds up his two front hoofs. 'She's in capable hoofs.'

I'm just about to grab hold of Barry's phosphorous rhinoceros nose-horn and climb aboard my high-tech armchair when I turn round, look Jim square in the eye, and say: 'You think you're funny, but you're not, you're just a cunt.'

'Eh?'

'That's right, Jim. A cunt.'

I stand here for a moment, waiting for him to hoof me, or put me down with one of his big giraffe-shaped put-downs, but he doesn't. He gives me a look, a peeved look, goes back into the house.